Snowbound on Skye

KATE LLOYD

UNION BAY PUBLISHING

"SKYE BOAT SONG,"
TRADITIONAL SCOTTISH SONG

Speed, bonnie boat, like a bird on a wing,
Onward! the sailors cry.
Carry the lad that's born to be king
Over the sea to Skye.

Though the waves leap, soft shall ye sleep;
Ocean's a royal bed.
Rocked in the deep, flora will keep
Watched by your weary head.

Speed, bonnie boat, like a bird on a wing,
Onward! the sailors cry.
Carry the lad that's born to be king
Over the sea to Skye.

Many's the lad fought on that day
Well the claymore could wield.
When the night came, silently lay
Dead on Culloden's field.

Speed, bonnie boat, like a bird on a wing,
Onward! the sailors cry.
Carry the lad that's born to be king
Over the sea to Skye.

Burned are our homes, exile and death
Scatter the loyal men.
Yet, 'ere the sword cool in the sheath
Charlie will come again!

Speed, bonnie boat, like a bird on a wing,
Onward! the sailors cry.
Carry the lad that's born to be king
Over the sea to Skye.

Dedicated to my father,
the late Prof. John Brodie McDiarmid

Chapter 1

Ever since the recent death of her parents, Denny was in a daze. *Unbelievable* was the word that looped through her mind like a never-ending figure eight. Denny still had to shake her head and remind herself that her parents were gone forever. And the drunk or stoned driver who forced them off the road was still at large. Road rage? Nothing made sense.

Denny raked her fingers through her tangled shoulder-length hair. Sometimes life wasn't fair. Well, what was she talking about? It never was.

Standing in her cozy bookstore before opening, she brought out a feather duster and got busy. Most of the used books were still in good shape. Many looked to be brand new and unread. Like her three copies of *War and Peace*, which Denny didn't find that long once she got into it. She liked to think the customers loved the books as much as she did.

But she would soon have to give up the business—just like her father had warned her. Too much overhead and not enough customers. It wasn't the first time Denny had what her father called a *Pie in the Sky* idea. As a child she'd set up a lemonade stand, washed neighbors' cars, and started a gardening service: weeding and mowing using her parents' mower until it ran out of gasoline. In the end her endeavors had all petered out. Denny didn't think she was lazy, but every business venture had failed. Bad weather, homework, or if honest with herself, yearning to look cool and wanting to spend time with boys had been the causes of her failures. Or was she fooling herself?

She checked her watch. Time to open. Where was Agnes, her one employee?

Her phone rang, startling her out of her musings. It was her only sibling, Maureen, calling—a rarity for her older sister, the always busy and famous cooking show diva.

"Is your passport up to date?" Maureen asked first thing.

"Yeah, I think so. Why?" Denny loved her sister with all her heart, but they led different lifestyles. Maureen didn't understand what it was like to be single and own a floundering business.

"I have a big surprise for you," Maureen said. "We're going to the Isle of Skye, off the west coast of Scotland, the land of our ancestors. And you're coming with us."

Denny didn't like surprises or being told what to do. "I can't afford to go anywhere." That was the truth.

"Don't you want to see the land of our ancestors—all expenses paid? My treat. Please say yes. James won't go with me."

"I can't leave my bookstore."

"Sure, you can. You have Agnes, don't you?"

Denny wanted to travel to Scotland someday, but she'd hoped on her honeymoon. Fat chance of that happening.

The bookstore's front door creaked open. Agnes straggled in, late as usual. Her mousy hair was matted on one side, and her clothes needed ironing, but Denny wouldn't complain. These days it was hard to find employees in a small town in rural New Jersey. She smiled at Agnes as she tried to think of ways to squirm out of Maureen's invitation.

If only their mother was still alive to consult with. But Mom would probably say, "Go, already. When was the last time you did something with your big sister?"

"Why the Isle of Skye?" Denny asked, her mind a battleground.

"I read an article about Skye in a travel magazine. It looks fabulous. A friend went there on a tour and had an awesome time."

"I'll think about it," Denny said. "When are you leaving?"

2

"Tomorrow."

"Uh, I couldn't possibly be ready." Denny didn't appreciate the bulldozer pressure.

"Just throw clothes into a suitcase, and you're good to go."

Denny's head spun with indecision as if she were a child balancing on a teeter-totter. "Yeah, okay, I guess." By the morning she'd feign sickness because a trip with Maureen wouldn't mend their fractured relationship.

Chapter 2

Denise Campbell cringed. She had no idea why hearing her older sister Maureen's crooning "Speed bonnie boat, like a bird on the wing over the sea to Skye," bugged her so much. Maureen had a lovely alto voice, but everything she'd said or did irritated Denny since they'd boarded the jet in Newark, New Jersey. And their father had hated this song for some unknown reason. He'd taken his distaste for the lyrics to his grave.

But Denny dared not complain since Maureen was paying for everything—first-class tickets, a five-star hotel—and had planned the whole trip. But this pint-size ferry boat was too freaky. A wave could tip it over.

Amanda, Maureen's fourteen-year-old daughter, stood a few feet away with Lydia, her Amish nanny, whom Maureen had insisted on bringing. The twenty-three-year-old wasn't dressed Amish, and her hair was lobbed short. When Denny asked Maureen about it, her sister confided that Lydia Fisher was jumping the fence—leaving the Amish community to live as an *Englischer*, meaning like everyone else in the United States. Maureen said she'd taught Lydia how to drive a car and helped her obtain a driver's license and a passport. Even allowed her to watch TV and use the internet. Things that were *verboten* for the Amish, according to Maureen, who'd called Denise Denny so long that it had stuck. Pretty much everyone did. Not that Denny minded all that much.

Chilly gusts of salty wind bit into Denny's cheeks. She was glad she was wearing her fleece jacket, but she'd neglected the gloves that were packed away at the bottom of her carry-on. Her fingers felt like icicles. No, that was wrong. She couldn't even feel them.

She'd read in a travel book at the shop that there was a bridge erected nearby, but Maureen had insisted they take the ferry. The old-fashioned way. No use arguing with Maureen.

Pulling her shoulder length hair back out of her eyes, Denny listened to gulls circling the small ferry's bow as she let random thoughts zigzag in her head. Maureen had everything, including a husband, a cute and spunky teen daughter, and a celebrity job, while Denny remained single. She'd given up searching for a husband who would take care of her, meaning a man she could confide in and let her rest her weary head on his shoulder. Denny had decided she would be content to remain childless and single for the rest of her life. If she told herself that often enough, she might believe it.

At least she owned her own business, a used bookstore that brought in a pittance. But Denny was proud of her accomplishments. Not that her sister or father had shared her pride. Still, she missed him. Greatly. And of course, her mother. She missed Mom every day of the week.

Maureen had always been the favorite child, but what did it matter now? And Maureen's husband was a creep as far as Denny was concerned. He'd had the gall to make a pass at Denny— several times. But she never complained for fear of causing a rift between Maureen and herself. Denny's best guess was that he wanted to get rid of her. He didn't like feisty Denny hanging around his complacent, gullible wife. No use saying anything negative about her husband. Maureen would plug her ears and refuse to believe it. As far as Maureen was concerned, her husband was perfect, even though Denny knew the truth. James was a lying, cheating SOB who would say or do anything to win a case. That's why women whose husbands had cheated on them flocked to him. And he had proven himself to be a winner. Raked in the dough for his clients.

Choppy water bounced the little ferry like a toy in a swimming pool with a dozen kids diving in. Denny gripped the railing. Her biggest trepidation was that she would die childless without a husband to love her. She had never shared her fears with anyone and never would. But when she thought about it, she should have feared that her parents would die prematurely. Way before expected. Her head still gyrated at the inconceivable reality. She'd felt like an orphan ever since their demise.

Chapter 3

Maureen should be having the time of her life, but her splendidly crafted world had shattered when two of the contestants on her primo cooking show fell ill right on the set and were carted off to the nearest emergency room. Someone had it in for her was all she could think. Right after that dreadful incident, the TV network asked her to take a two-week sabbatical.

As the mini ferryboat vaulted along, she wondered if she should have taken her contestants flowers or make some sort of amends. Feeling responsible, she could have visited them at the hospital where they'd spent the night. But the network's leadership would not hear of it. "Keep a low profile" were their instructions. "You haven't taken a vacation in years."

"But I don't want a vacation." What would Maureen do with herself? Where would she go?

"Let's wait for this to blow over." He'd folded his arms across his barrel of a chest. "If it does."

Was he thinking that the sight of Maureen would make the two contestants sick enough to drop dead or incur a lawsuit? She knew her eight o'clock Friday night spot was coveted by many. Did one of her rivals have it in for her?

A trip with her husband and daughter had seemed like the best distraction. Somewhere peaceful and relaxing.

"No way" had blasted from James's mouth as if he were in the courtroom when she'd asked him to accompany her. "I have a business to run and cases to handle. I can't just leave on a whim." Her big-shot attorney husband always had something

7

more important to do than to spend time with Maureen and their daughter, Amanda, so she should be used to it by now. He was devoted to his clients. They always came first. Just thinking about his reaction sent jabs of pain through her chest and abdomen like sharp scissors, but she would not complain. She was used to keeping her thoughts and disappointments to herself.

It wasn't as if Maureen hadn't contributed to their family's income for the past five years. James had griped often enough about what a high tax bracket they were in because of her job. He might be thrilled silly if she got fired.

A gull swooped so low that Maureen bent at the waist. The obnoxious bird was no doubt on the prowl for food and garbage. Maureen never used to be so timid. But everything seemed to be going wrong.

She wondered if her TV program would be permanently canceled by the time she got home. A cooking diva with a program called *Marvelous Maureen's Menu*. Would she be replaced by a younger, prettier woman? Or would her husband do that first? He had a roving eye, but now was not the time to fret about him.

Ordinarily, she would have called her mother for advice. But no longer was Mom available. That grizzly truth spiked into Maureen again.

Only weeks before her show's debacle both of her parents died. She could barely stand to think of it, so she pushed the gruesome images aside.

Mom had been a blonde head-turner who'd retained her svelte looks to the end, thanks to her beauty salon and plastic surgeon. In her younger years, people had said Maureen was the spitting image of her gorgeous mother. But Maureen had nibbled a few too many desserts. She had to sample what was prepared on TV, didn't she? She might go on a diet and sign up for that exercise class their neighbor recommended when she got home.

The ferry bobbed across the steely gray sea. The clouds hung so low they melded with the water, and her feet were cold.

8

Not a place James would have chosen. She was glad he wasn't here to berate her, but she could hear his voice in her head.

"Who in their right mind would want to go to the Isle of Skye this time of year?" he'd asked, as if she'd planned to hop aboard a rocket ship headed to Mars. "Now St. Andrews might be a different story... No, I don't even have time for golf with my workload."

Didn't he understand she was grieving for the loss of her parents? He'd attended the memorial service but did little more.

Maureen glanced down at Amanda, who wore a frown on her face. Thank goodness Maureen had thought to bring her daughter's cheerful nanny, Lydia, a twenty-three-year-old Amish beauty.

Maureen inhaled to her fullest and tried to appreciate the salty air while her stomach soured. Standing at the bow of the boat, she caught sight of the island through the mist, and her heart filled with gladness. She vowed to let nothing stand in the way of her temporary happiness. Not even Denny would rattle her, nor Amanda, who was often lippy and unappreciative. Maureen knew she had spoiled the girl rotten but too late to fix that now. She hoped her younger sister and Lydia would be a good influence on Amanda. And on Maureen. Distract her from her many losses anyway.

Chapter 4

Lydia breathed in the pungent, briny air, glad to be at sea-level again and moving at a slow speed, even though the water was rough, and the wind tossed her bobbed hair. She watched the frothy bubbles floating on the water's surface.

Ach. She felt a surge of nausea and tasted bile in the back of her throat. She had never ridden on anything larger than a rowboat in her parents' pond out behind the barn. She affixed her vision on the shore ahead—not that far away she assured herself. The buggies back in Gordonville were this bouncy, and she never got sick.

Lydia let out an extended sigh. She missed the intoxicating farmland aromas of newly turned soil and of warm leather bridles. But not of mucking out the milking cows' stalls, a chore she was always saddled with. She missed standing alongside her *mam* in the kitchen canning but not washing the never-ending sinks of dirty dishes. Why didn't her brothers have to wash dishes? Maureen had an electric dishwasher that washed and dried the glasses and dishes until they sparkled. Sure, Lydia had to do a little scraping every now and then, but her workload was greatly reduced. For instance, she could toss dirty clothes in the washing machine and then the dryer instead of hanging them on a laundry line. This past winter on the farm she'd hung them in her parents' basement to dry. It seemed as though she was stuck with every chore. Yet she missed the unique fragrance of sun-dried sheets. A splash of Downy Fabric Softener couldn't compare.

Gulls circled overhead, screeching, sounding like sirens. An ill omen?

Their cries admonished her for leaving home without a word. She felt like crying for her disobedience but reminded herself that this was a chance of a lifetime. Amanda was a challenge, but Lydia had grown fond of the girl. Lydia often wished she could act like a spoiled brat too. Stomp her feet and scream the way Amanda did when her anger boiled over like a pot of oatmeal when the gas stove was set too high. Throw a tantrum.

Lydia recalled their trip earlier today to reach this distant point—what time was it anyway? She'd never been allowed to wear a wristwatch and wondered what time it was back in Lancaster County. Was *Dat* doing the morning or afternoon milking? Had Jonathan come over to help him? Were they talking about her? Was Jonathan asking *Dat* if he would allow Lydia to marry him or had Jonathan already found another woman to court?

A gull holding a piece of trash in its bill swooped past her. She grasped the railing, ducked her head. She had been surprised that she was not terrified on the flight over the Atlantic Ocean with nothing but thin air holding her up. Except for takeoff, she had been too preoccupied with Amanda, who'd demanded to go to the bathroom minutes before liftoff and accepting drinks and trays of food from the flight attendants. Who would have thought that she would have been so fussed over in an airplane? Not that she had been able to doze off as some of the passengers did. Men and women probably on their way to an important meeting and had popped sleeping pills in their mouths and dozed off like rag dolls.

Lydia was used to catering to others. Her job in the family had been to care for other people's needs before her own. At home she'd been taught to serve others first and had been rebuked when she hadn't. The second to the youngest of ten children, she was used to being last in line. And her parents demanded respect. Particularly after her father was chosen by lot to be minister of their district. *Ach*, what he must think of her now.

11

Maybe her parents didn't know. It's not as if they were allowed to carry cell phones in their pockets. Although somehow news traveled through the Amish community as fast as a rock in a slingshot. Her friends might have caught wind of this trip—and then told another and then another.

She rubbed her hands together for warmth. She was glad she was wearing her black winter coat and mittens and a blue scarf wrapped around her neck. Maureen had lent her a red crocheted beanie for the occasion. Maureen had hinted that Lydia should bundle up for this trip, and she was glad she'd listened. Nothing she would have worn back home, but the beanie was warming her ears. Her white heart-shaped cap would have blown off in the wind and as would her black winter hat.

Where was Amanda? Lydia reminded herself that this was not a pleasure trip. She was an employee looking after a scrappy girl who adored instigating trouble. Amanda delighted in it.

Lydia hadn't let on that she knew Amanda had been put on probation and possibly would be asked not to return to her expensive preppy school after her vacation. Lydia never would have dared misbehave at her one room schoolhouse. Or at home.

Ach, she was tired of being obedient.

She heard chatter and noticed passengers were shuffling to the handful of cars. Since the four of them had arrived by bus and walked aboard, they would be met by a local driver whom Maureen had hired for a week to chauffeur them to their hotel and then around the island. How exciting.

"Where's my daughter?" Maureen startled Lydia out of her musings. Maureen wore an expression of fear, her eyes wide and the corners of her mouth pulled back.

"She was here a moment ago." Lydia looked around but did not see the girl. "She must be somewhere."

Maureen let out a huff. "I brought you along to look after her." Maureen's voice turned frantic. "What if she fell overboard? What if she was kidnapped? Things like that happen."

"I'm sorry, I'll find her." Lydia felt a jarring sensation and heard men speaking. She realized the small ferry must be docking. This was exactly like one of Amanda's many strategies to rattle her mother. Lydia would not be surprised if Amanda had disembarked the ferry by herself just to garner her mother's attention.

"You go this way, and I'll go that way," Maureen said. "And Denny, please, please, please, won't you make sure she doesn't get off with the cars?"

"Yes, ma'am, big sister." Denny gave Maureen a mock salute. Lydia detected an eye roll behind Denny's dark sunglasses.

"I'll thank you not to call me big again," Maureen snapped.

Denny didn't apologize. "As if you didn't call me a shrimp when I was young?"

Maureen seemed to be holding in a mouthful of barbed words.

"I'll bet Amanda's in the ladies' room, wherever that is." Denny looked around.

"Good thought." Maureen pivoted to Lydia and said, "Find the ladies' room or whatever they call it here."

"*Yah*, okay, right away." Lydia dashed off to do as told. Sure enough, in a room with a Toilet sign affixed to the door, she found Amanda peering in the mirror and slathering on makeup. Amanda stopped for a moment and then set about applying eyeliner and mascara. She looked five years older. Lydia wouldn't mind wearing makeup too. She might even ask Amanda for a lesson on how to apply it. But not now.

Maureen must have seen Lydia's expression as she swung open the door wider and said, "What's keeping you, honey?"

"I had to go to the bathroom, Mommy."

Maureen's eyes bulged. "You scared me half to death."

"Gosh, don't freak out. Can't I have a little privacy?"

Lydia was thankful that Amanda didn't belt out a swear word. The girl was certainly capable of it. And right now, she looked like a woman of the night—an expression her parents had used. Whatever that meant. Lydia marveled at Amanda's transformation and then reminded herself that her parents would think the same thing of her, what with her new hairdo and skinny jeans. She was relieved they weren't here. *Ach*, her *dat* would call her short hair an abomination.

A thought hit Lydia like a poison dart. She might never see her family again. One thousand visions hurdled through her brain. She doubted she would be shunned if she returned and asked for forgiveness. Her parents and the community would grant her that. But the plane could crash on the way home, or some other gruesome tragedy might occur. She doubted Maureen or Denny would save her. Their attention would be fixed upon Amanda as it should be.

"Be anxious for nothing," one of the ministers had said at church last year. She admonished herself for worrying, a pastime that had plagued her since childhood.

Wasn't she aching for a new adventure? Yes. Even if it meant dying to achieve it.

Chapter 5

Denny had to chuckle. Amanda's pranks reminded her of her own shenanigans when she was a girl. She had done everything to get her parents' attention. Wasted energy because they always focused on Maureen's achievements. Maureen's over-the-top wedding. Maureen's baby girl, their one and only grandchild. Maureen's wildly successful TV show. Nothing Denny did could compete.

They were gone now forever, but she couldn't stop thinking about them, like a never-ending loop. She wished she could shut off her brain. A song her mother used to play haunted her now. "You don't know what you've got till it's gone." Denny couldn't remember the rest of the words, just the beginning over and over and over again.

As she stepped toward the exit, she noticed a fellow standing below on shore. Nothing like a regular American man as he was wearing a tartan cap and carrying a sign with the name Mrs. Cook written on it.

"There's our driver," Maureen said, all abuzz and waving her hand like a weirdo. "Hello there. I'm Mrs. Cook." He boarded the ferry, and she strode over and shook his hand.

"Welcome to the Isle of Skye." The man spoke with a distinct Scottish accent. Denny had to wonder if it was fabricated for tourists. In any case, he was hot. About her age, meaning thirty-two. And trim. Not all that tall, but she could tell he was muscled under his tweed jacket. Denny figured he was probably married or had a girlfriend. She tried to spot a wedding band, but he was wearing leather gloves—what she should be doing. She was glad she'd brought a pair, but they were in the bottom of her suitcase.

His dreamy hazel-brown eyes caught hers for a moment, and then he gazed at Lydia longer than seemed necessary. Lydia blushed and looked away.

Next, he turned to Amanda. "And who is this lovely young lass?" He put out his hand to shake Amanda's in a chivalrous manner.

"My daughter, Amanda," Maureen said. "Under all that makeup is a fourteen-year-old girl."

Amanda gave her mother the evil eye. Not that Denny blamed her. When would Maureen figure it out? But of course, Denny said nothing. She was determined not to tangle with her sister the whole trip. Probably an impossible feat.

"May I introduce myself?" The man tipped his cap. "I'm Alec MacLeod. I'm glad you chose to ride the ferry today as there was a hideous accident on the bridge, making it impossible to cross."

"What was it?" Fear clutched Denny as she imagined the worst-case scenario.

"A passenger bus skidded on the black ice."

Maureen's hand rose to her mouth, but she said nothing. Denny figured Maureen was worried about possible fatalities— and also remembering their parents' death, just as Denny was.

Denny finally spoke since all the other women seemed in a daze. "Good to meet you," she said, shaking his hand. "I'm Denny Campbell."

"A Campbell on Skye? Best keep that fact tucked under your cap as they say."

"And why is that?" She was in the mood to flirt. She wished she'd taken a glance at herself in the mirror in the ladies' room earlier. But too late now. She was sure she looked disheveled at best. And her frigid ears must be beet-red. "Well?"

"Nothing, I shouldn't have said anything." He repositioned his cap revealing wavy brick-red hair. "A long-standing feud that should end as of today."

"Or what? You'll drive us over a cliff?" Not that she would mind it all that much. After going to her gynecologist repeatedly and having every test in the book, Denny wondered if death awaited her like a ticking time bomb. Cancer was most likely lurking in her, but her doctors couldn't locate it. Most likely in an ovary was Denny's guess. Like a wet dog, she tried to shake the grisly feeling off and made the decision not to dwell on her health again all week.

"Absolutely not." His cheeks grew flushed. "I promise to take the very best care of four such beauties as you."

Amanda giggled as if he had spoken directly to her. She was morphing into a young woman way too fast in Denny's opinion.

Denny rubbed her hands together. "Is it always this cold?" Even though she was shivering, she was grateful for the distraction. She needed to stop grieving for her parents, although that might never come to an end. A gloomy thought. And to stop worrying about her health.

She reminded herself that she must call her bookshop and speak to Agnes. But it wouldn't be open yet. She liked to think it could run without her. Yet Denny wondered if Agnes would open on time. And remember to make the deposit and to complete one hundred different tasks such as check for stray books that customers had stuck in the wrong section.

Let's see, how many hours behind was New Jersey anyway? Her mind walked itself backward eight hours. No wonder she was so tired. She hadn't slept a wink on the jet. A multitude of fears had clutched her. The jet's crashing, pulling apart, and sinking to the bottom of the ocean. Death might be a relief. It had beckoned her for years. Putting up a brave front while in pain was exhausting. She hadn't told anyone about her many gynecologist and gastroenterologist appointments. "Go on the trip and enjoy yourself," her ob-gyn had said. "We'll tackle the health situation when you get home." Easy for her to say.

Denny couldn't confide in her mother when Mom was alive. She hadn't for years. And Maureen would multiply Denny's fears by pummeling her with questions. She always did. Like a prosecutor at a trial. Her inquiries multiplied and enlarged the situation. Even if she were asking why Denny ate organic veggies and fruit when they were so expensive. Poor Amanda.

"Ladies, may I take you to my car?" Alec's voice with its lovely Scottish brogue and rolled *r*'s brought her back to reality. She needed to wake up and dive into this time zone. He led them to his forest-green sedan and opened a back door. "I'm afraid someone will have to sit up front with me."

"I will, I will." Amanda said and jumped into the front seat much to Denny's consternation. She was hoping to claim that spot herself.

"Hey, you're sitting on the wrong side," Denny told her niece.

"She is not," Maureen scolded.

"Oh, yeah." Denny felt like an idiot. "Sorry, Amanda."

"No worries," Amanda said. "You're still my favorite aunt."

"Your only aunt," Maureen said.

Alec directed his words at Denny. "You'll get used to how we do things in no time at all," he said.

Denny wondered if she could drive on the wrong side of the road. Not that it was wrong here in Scotland. The British Isles that is.

"It's a short drive." He glanced into the back seat for a moment, and his gaze caught Denny's. "Tomorrow, I'll take you anywhere on the island you like." He provided each of them a map and a pamphlet with information about the Isle of Skye. "I am at your command all week." He scanned the horizon. "Unless it snows. Sometimes it does."

"Snow in February?" Maureen's voice reminded Denny of a parrot's squawk. "What are you talking about?"

His eyebrows lifted. "It rarely snows on Skye at all, but every decade or so we get some this time of year. It's predicted in the weather forecast."

"Goody, goody, we can go skiing like I wanted to back home." Amanda clapped her hands.

"I can't imagine we'll get enough snow to ski." Alec ignited the engine. "But it does sound fun." He released the parking brake. "Also, a wee bit of a headache for cars without studded tires—like mine."

In ways, Denny wished they had their own car, but she'd agreed with Maureen that driving on the wrong side of the road would be possible only if the driver kept their concentration on driving all the time and didn't admire the view for even an instant. Having a hired driver who knew the area would be better. Anyway, why tangle with Maureen when she would come out victorious eventually. She always had for Denny's whole life. Denny had continually wanted to be like her big sister, pathetic as it may sound. But as Denny admired Alec's even features, she decided being single had its advantages. If Alec was single and available, that is.

Never would she admit that her former boyfriend, Kevin, had dumped her like stale bread the day after her parents' memorial service. He hadn't even supported her as a friend when she'd needed him most. Maybe all men were cads, and she'd expected too much.

"This hotel is a perfect location." Alec drove them to an exquisite four-story building that made all at home look drab. "You'll be a twenty-minute walk from Portree, Skye's biggest town. See the lights way down there?" He got out and opened Denny's door first, then jogged around to the other side to open Maureen's. Her older sister looked displeased. Denny should warn her that scowling would give her permanent wrinkles but decided to let her be grumpy. If anything, seeing her older sister's glower brought Denny pleasure. The first time since their parents' demise that she was thinking about others, even if in a nasty sense. Maureen drove her bonkers sometimes.

Alec opened his sedan's doors. Denny's first—which brought her pleasure. She enjoyed the attention even if he was only doing his job. Then he circled the car and assisted Maureen, followed by Lydia. Amanda hopped out on her own.

19

Denny stared up at the hotel's imposing facade. Not what she had expected of Scotland, which she assumed would be lackluster and downright plain. She glanced over to Lydia, who was also standing with her jaw dropped open in awe of the structure. The setting sun cast a peach-colored glow across the hotel's surface.

"Nice enough, Denny?" Maureen leaned against Denny.

"It looks w-wonderful." Denny contained any bitter words that might slip out. She knew she had a sharp tongue and didn't want Alec to think she was a grump. The sky was growing dark as a mattress of clouds rolled in. But no matter. They'd be inside soon and hopefully warm up. Denny zipped her jacket to her neck as a gust of wind brought with it icy air.

Alec pulled open the hotel's massive front door. "Care to enter, madam?" He spoke to Maureen. "I'll fetch the luggage in a moment."

Clutching her purse with FENDI proudly embossed on its leather surface, Maureen strode into the foyer like a queen entering her castle. Denny knew her older sister was a TV star, so she guessed Maureen was used to being in the spotlight. And Denny told herself she wasn't jealous of her anymore.

But when it came to looks, why had Denny gleaned their father's dark, stout DNA while Maureen had inherited their mother's long legs and blonde hair?

20

Chapter 6

Maureen had expected James to phone or text her by now, but she swatted the thoughts away as if they were pesky gnats. He rarely called her when she was home, so why would he change his modus operandi now? But he might worry about Amanda just this once. An early riser, her husband might already be at the gym. He loved to be the first one there. And everywhere.

She calculated the time back home and decided that not even James would get up this early. She wondered if he was sleeping in his own bed. With her out of town, anything could happen. Many mornings she woke up and found him snoozing in the guest room. He'd explained that he didn't want to bother her when he got home so late from a meeting and then buzzed off to work early—when the stock market opened. But she had to wonder.

She felt disconnected from him. An unsettling thought hit her like an arrow flying out of nowhere: did he love her anymore? And did she care. No matter. Now was not the time to wrestle with such monumental questions. Not when an adventure awaited her.

She checked in her purse to make sure her phone was there, then chided herself for thinking James might have called her when her phone was on airplane mode.

"Everything okay, sis?" Denny asked her.

"Just checking to make sure I didn't forget anything."

"Don't worry, we're in good hands with Alec." Denny elongated his name in a lazy way that made Maureen think Denny had set her sight on him. "He seems trustworthy."

Honestly, couldn't Denny keep her priorities in check? Maureen had not brought her little sister along to troll for men.

Chapter 7

Lydia trailed Denny, Maureen, and Amanda into the beautiful hotel. She couldn't help but gawk. She had never seen such splendor. Ahead a fire crackled in an enormous hearth as tall as she was, not that she was all that tall. Off to the left, an older woman stood behind a counter with a young man, welcoming new arrivals. While Maureen checked them in using a credit card, Lydia admired the many works of art and the furniture upholstered with what must be nothing but the finest brocade cloth. Not like what she'd seen in Amish homes or fabric stores back in Lancaster County.

A hotel employee, a middle-aged woman, clad in a velveteen vest and a plaid kilt, offered them refreshments while Alec brought in the luggage. Lydia had noticed that his gaze had lingered on her, but she had paid him little attention. Something about his demeanor made her nervous. Her father had always told her to beware of men. She reminded herself she was wearing skinny jeans. What did she expect when she was flaunting her body like a... She couldn't even say the word. Her parents would be outraged. She was glad they couldn't see her.

Feeling lightheaded, she sank down onto a high-back chair and appreciated the cushy surface that was so unlike the wooden benches she perched upon at church. No more wooden chairs for a whole week. Or maybe forever as far as she was concerned.

"Welcome to the MacDonald Hotel." A woman wearing a plaid kilt and carrying a tray smiled at her. "Care for a drink of bubbly?"

23

"*Yah*—okay." Lydia accepted a fluted glass. She knew this was champagne, an alcoholic drink her parents would not approve of, but she took a sip anyway. The bubbles went right to her head, which was already spinning from drowsiness. Not that she hadn't drunk alcoholic beverages before, even though she realized she was sinning. It wasn't her first and worst sin. But she did not wish to admit it in front of the congregation. The thought of living a blameless life was too much of a burden. With a minister for a father, she would never be free.

She placed her glass on a table then dropped her other hand over the side of the chair and felt something cool on her fingertips. Startled, she sat up straight and peered over the side. A scruffy little dog that reminded her of a neighbor's pup back in Lancaster County smiled up at her.

"Piper is that you?" she asked, and the dog let out a demure yap.

"No barking," said one of the waitresses in a firm voice. "Sorry, miss," she said to Lydia.

"Not a problem. I love dogs." Lydia scratched the dog's furry head. "She reminds me of my neighbor's cairn terrier, Piper, only lighter in color. And this one seems quite a bit broader around the middle."

"She's soon to whelp her pups." The waitress, also donning a tartan kilt, smoothed her hand over the dog's extended abdomen. "Any day now according to the veterinarian."

"What's her name?"

"Princess. Because most of the time she acts like one. But she's not allowed in the dining area. Our patrons wouldn't like it. Nor would the health inspector." The waitress extracted a treat from a pocket and bent over. Princess sprang to life with ears pricked and tail wagging. "Come along with me, naughty girl, you know you're not allowed out here."

Lydia wished there were a way to bring one of the puppies home with her. Not that she really had a home anymore. She felt the weight of loneliness she'd experienced much of her life, even when surrounded by her parents and her extended family—*Mam* and *Dat*, siblings, cousins, and grandparents.

24

"Cairn terriers were originally from this island." The waitress sounded proud. "They were bred to root out vermin from what we call cairns—heaps of stones."

"Really?" Lydia wondered if the young woman was pulling her leg.

"Who's this little cutie?" Denny spoke over the waitress's shoulder. Princess turned her full attention to Denny, who extended her hand. Princess licked her fingers and wagged her tail as if they were old friends.

"Her name is Princess, and she's having puppies any day now." Lydia couldn't contain her excitement.

"Maybe in the wee hours of the night tonight according to the veterinarian." The waitress turned to Denny. "She obviously likes you," she said.

"I adore dogs." Denny scratched Princess behind her ears.

"Maybe you should bring a puppy home with you," Lydia said, thinking of herself.

"I imagine the pups will be the cutest ever." Denny rubbed her chin. "But I wouldn't be able to give it the attention it deserves." Her voice didn't sound convincing, but Lydia was too shy to speak up, to say that she wanted a puppy for herself.

And maybe a man like Alec. If she stayed here in Scotland, perhaps she could have both.

Chapter 8

Denny covered her yawning mouth. She couldn't blame her fatigue on jet lag alone. She'd been sleep-deprived ever since her parents' death. She'd been besieged with nightmares and crushing feelings of guilt. Not that she had anything to feel guilty about. But still, if she'd offered to drive her parents' home from the opera that night or ordered them an Uber, they'd still be alive.

Her thoughts meandered to her little bookstore with its front bay window and tall bookcases crammed with mostly used but also some new books. How would it survive without her there for a whole week? She chastised herself for agreeing to come on this trip just to make her older sister happy. Her whole life she'd followed in her big sister's footsteps. Never quite as good. Never as successful. Maureen was a star while Denny was stuck in her dumb meager life. And as far as she could tell, she might not live another year. She shouldn't have gone on any trip until she'd found out what was wrong with her. Pain in her abdomen had been warning her for over a year. Yet her gynecologist, after performing a series of tests, had found nothing. That doctor sent her to a gastroenterologist, who had finally turned her over to an oncologist, who suggested she try counseling. Which made Denny angry. What a nerve. Her pain was real. Not all in her head.

Denny was tempted to call Agnes to find out if the young woman had opened the store but figured it was still too early. With Denny out of town would she bother coming to work at all? When it came down to it, did it matter? Business had been so slow Denny could barely pay the rent, insurance, and Agnes's wages.

Dad had been right when he'd ridiculed Denny's selling used books. But it was her passion. She knew she needed to buy more stock and to advertise. She'd toyed with the idea of branching out and offering gifts. But what? Since her parents' death, it felt as if she were crossing a river, the current pushing her downstream, her footing unsure on the slippery rocks.

As Denny surveyed the hotel's grand decor, she pulled her mind back to the present. Since she'd told Maureen that she would go along with anything she had planned, Denny couldn't complain. And this hotel looked fancy-schmancy. She envisioned herself sinking into a bed with a soft pillow and smooth sheets. All she wanted was a good night's sleep, but her doctor had refused to give her sleeping pills. Maybe Maureen had a sleep aid. Perhaps she also suffered from insomnia. There was so much Denny didn't know about her only sibling. Not that Maureen knew much about Denny, who kept her secret safely tucked away.

Chapter 9

"Your parents called and left a message," a woman at the hotel's front desk told Maureen as she produced her credit card. "They're running late."

"That's impossible." Maureen was flummoxed. "There's some mistake."

"I took the call myself." The young woman sounded sincere.

Denny moved over to the front desk. "Believe me when I tell you they will not be coming. Because they are dead." Denny spoke in a matter-of-fact manner that irked Maureen to no end. "They're deader than dead. Dead as a doorknob." She turned to Maureen and asked, "Were they ever planning to come on this trip with us?"

"No."

"Did you ever invite them?"

"No, not that I recall." Maureen wanted to tell her to shut up. But there was no shutting up her little sister. Her little sister had the zaniest ideas, but Maureen would support her this time. They shared a common loss. They were both orphans, no matter their age.

Maureen generated the cheerful facade she wore when on the show's production set as she signed her name and reinserted her card into her wallet. She felt her world spinning out of control. She wished Denny would not speak about their death ever again. Even thinking about their memorial service made Maureen want to gag, as Amanda would say. She had come here to forget about that and everything else.

"How on earth could this happen?" Maureen asked.

The corner of Denny's mouth lifted on one side. "I'll bet this is one of Jimbo's little pranks that are never funny."

Denny was right about his often-tasteless humor.

"If you're referring to my husband, you know he hates being called that. His name is James." He despised even being called Jim.

"Don't get your tail in a knot, Sis."

"Why in heaven's name would James do a thing like that?" As Maureen waited for an explanation, she asked herself why she'd invited Denny on this trip to begin with. She glanced over to see her daughter hugging her Aunt Denny around the waist. Lydia was staring at her with a look of confusion. As were all the other guests in the foyer.

It seemed their whole lives, Denny had tried without success to emulate Maureen. It wasn't Maureen's fault that she was older and that she worked her tail off to get good grades. Or that the camera loved her. Things didn't always come easy for Maureen, but she persevered. And she also knew how to manipulate people. Yes, she admitted it to herself. She was manipulative. After all, how did she ensnare James in college? Not that he was the catch of the century.

"May I show you to your rooms now?" a twenty-something lass asked Maureen. "Welcome, I'm Molly." The vivacious young woman dressed in a kilt glanced to Alec and grinned. "Hi there, handsome," she said, sweet as honey.

Alec spoke to Maureen's entourage. "I assume you'll have supper and breakfast in the hotel. The food here is impossible to beat." He spoke directly to Denny. "See you in the morning." And then next he said, "I hope you all sleep well." He turned to leave. "Goodnight."

"Good night." Amanda's smudged makeup had transformed her face into a ghoulish clown, but she seemed oblivious, her attention set on Alec. "See you tomorrow."

Had her daughter suddenly become interested in older men?

Amanda had asked when she could start dating but had been told in no uncertain terms that she couldn't date until she was sixteen.

"Don't worry, there are a myriad of sights to see," he said as if he could read her thoughts. "We can decide over breakfast."

Lydia batted her eyelashes at him if Maureen was not mistaken. Had the young woman forgotten she was here to look after Amanda not flirt with the driver? Maureen would put a stop to this behavior. She spoke to Denny. "I'm putting you in the same room with Lydia, and Amanda will sleep with me."

"Mommy." Amanda spoke with a whine in her voice that betrayed her age. "I want to room with Aunt Denny.

"Not this trip." Maureen held firm instead of her usual flimsy cave-in to her daughter's demands.

"But you never let me do anything I want."

Maureen felt like laughing out loud. She knew her daughter was a spoiled brat, and here was more evidence. But she held her tongue and clamped her lips together.

"Please follow me." Molly escorted them up the grand carpeted staircase to the second floor.

Chapter 10

Lydia followed Molly, Denny, and Amanda up the stairs. As an employee, she assumed that was the right thing to do. Not that she couldn't have traveled at twice their speed. As she trod up the stairs, she came to grips with the fact that she and Denny were going to room together. Why Maureen wouldn't let her sleep with Amanda was beyond her comprehension.

To be fair, Lydia understood that Maureen wanted to spend time with her daughter. And it was about time. It seemed as though Maureen had too many other important commitments. Priorities more important than her daughter, which had baffled Lydia. What could be more important than family? She realized she was being judgmental. If family was so important, why had she left her own back in Lancaster County?

She'd heard an *Englisch* saying "familiarity breeds contempt." Deep inside did she harbor contempt for her family and the Amish community? She didn't think so and certainly hoped not. She hadn't made Jonathan her priority either. She hadn't written him as promised or contacted him for six months, for which she felt remorse. But not sorry enough to do anything about it. Too much explaining to do, and more opportunity for lies to burble out of her mouth. And she had heard that lying leads to more lies.

But now was not the time to become squeaky honest. Maureen might fire her and leave her here to fend for herself. With no family and Amish community, no husband to take care of her, and no job, how would she cope?

Chapter 11

Denny was wowed by her room. Nicer than any hotel suite she'd ever seen. She wondered how much her older sister was paying for it. A bundle no doubt. But she wouldn't ask and incur her sister's wrath. And what if Maureen suddenly decided to ask Denny to pay half? No way could Denny afford even a cheap motel room back home. Not that she'd have any need for one.

The porter had already brought her suitcase upstairs and set it on a chest at the foot of a single bed. A fire crackled in the fireplace and brocade fabric adorned the furniture.

"Which bed do you want?" she asked Lydia. Denny was still sizing up the beds, which were equally splendid with their extra pillows. Bed tables supported opulent lamps and what appeared to be original works of art adorned the walls covered with flowered wallpaper.

"I wouldn't know how to choose." Lydia looked around. "Everything is so beautiful."

Denny peered out the window and saw a body of water. She had to admit her sister was right about choosing this hotel. Not that she'd ever say anything to Maureen. Since their teens, they had held a rivalry, starting when Maureen had stolen her boyfriend. No, it was more than that. Maureen had always excelled at everything, whereas Denny had come in second place. She knew she needed to get over it, but she couldn't.

The door was still ajar. The young woman poked her head in. "Any questions for me before I leave? Remember my name is Molly. I am at your service until midnight."

Denny surveyed the fireplace with its glowing embers and

the split wood sitting in a brass container. "Molly, any way to warm up this room?"

"Sorry. It is unseasonably cold this year. We have a furnace. I'll turn up the heat." Molly's hand moved to the thermostat by the light switch near the door. "If you like, I can add wood to the fire."

"No, that's okay. We can handle that." The last thing Denny needed was to croak from affixation. Things like that happened according to the news, and she did not trust the smoke detector's battery. Who knew when it was last changed?

Denny was tempted to inquire why Campbells were unpopular on this island but would wait and ask Alec in the morning. Her father had always been proud of his Scottish heritage but had never expanded beyond the details and singing, "The Campbells are coming, hurrah!" He'd had a hearty baritone voice she could hear in her inner ear. For a moment, she was gripped by sadness and regret. She wished she'd spent more time listening to and appreciating him. But no use in thinking about it now. Her heritage would be something to talk about in the morning with Alec, but he seemed to have little interest in her.

She noticed a bookshelf laden with books and travel brochures. Perhaps she would find her answers there, but her eyes were too tired. All she wanted to do was crawl into bed and fall asleep, but she'd read that she would be best served by staying awake a few hours longer to beat jet lag. But not past midnight. Or had she gotten the instructions all mixed up?

Her mind spun back to reality. She thought of her bookstore, The Open Book, as her little baby, but she was on the brink of bankruptcy unless she came home with a whole new plan. That was one reason why she'd agreed to come on this trip. She hoped to find inspiration. She might as well consider it her baby since she doubted that she'd have any children of her own. Unless she adopted, a scenario she'd rehearsed in her mind often.

"I could help you put your clothes away," Lydia said.

"No, thanks, I can manage." Denny unzipped her carry-on.

"Really, I don't mind."

Denny did not want Lydia to see the contents of her carry-on. She'd tossed in her clothing and knew from Maureen's descriptions that Lydia was fastidious. A regular little neatnik when it came to house cleaning and ironing. "Go help Amanda and Maureen," Denny said to her.

Lydia seemed to come to life. "*Gut* idea." Snatching up her room key, she spun on her heel and headed out the door.

Denny brought out her cell phone but realized she had no one to call. In the past, she had spoken to her mother every day, but she had not appreciated the woman. Today she would do anything to hear her voice. Other than business acquaintances and her one employee, who were not really friends, who was left? Her friends from high school and college had all moved away. They had husbands and children. The stigma of being single at her age was humongous. Denny realized this was why she worked twelve-hour days. To avoid solitude. She should get herself a pet. She'd always been a dog lover but had decided she wasn't home enough. Maybe if she owned a dog like Princess, she'd stay at home more. Or bring the dog to work to keep her company.

"Knock, knock." Maureen spoke as she opened the door. "Let's go downstairs to the restaurant for supper. Alec said their food is to die for."

"I hope it doesn't kill us," Denny said, and Maureen cringed. "I meant compared to your cooking it will probably be so-so."

"Let's not mention that I'm a chef to anyone on the staff." Maureen's face showed genuine concern.

"And that you have your own TV show?" Denny was baffled. "In your fans' eyes, you're a superstar."

"Please don't mention it again on this trip, okay?"

"Whatever." Denny wondered what had come over her sister who usually adored basking in the spotlight, being the center of attention. She bet that during the meal Maureen Cook, the magnificent chef, would find a way to let the information slip out. Or maybe she figured someone sitting in the dining room would recognize her and ask for her autograph.

"Come as you are," Maureen said. "You always look beautiful."

"I don't feel it," Denny said in a rare moment of honesty. "Are you sure we shouldn't dress for supper?"

"Molly said to come as we are. Because the bridge is closed, several large tables of customers have canceled."

Denny glanced down at her slacks, then decided she didn't care what she looked like. Her shoulder-length brown hair was probably a mess but who cared? Lydia wasn't even wearing makeup, but she had that beautiful, always perfect complexion. Denny wondered what her story was and decided she would wait until after supper to find out. Maureen had told her Lydia was Amish. Denny housed a whole section of Amish romance novels in her bookstore; she had read only three and had decided they were fun. Maybe even inspiring. And shoppers had scooped them up as if they were made of gold.

Minutes later Denny, Lydia, Amanda, and Maureen ventured down the staircase. Molly directed them into the dining room. Denny stood for a moment, taking in the spacious area with two dozen tables. The settings were fantastic. Fine china and what Denny assumed was real silver-plated flatware.

The four women were seated at a window table overlooking a body of water. Maureen didn't divulge that she was a renowned chef. How very odd was all Denny could think. Her older sister usually found a way to mention herself, but Denny kept quiet. Her head spun with fatigue and jet lag. She admonished herself not to try to figure out what time it was at home or fret about her bookstore again. She was here, and she would dive into this time zone. She scanned the extensive menu and decided to pass on the haggis, which she'd read was chopped sheep's heart, liver, and lungs—yuck. Rather than act like a dumb tourist and remark about its bizarre ingredients she examined the menu again.

"Miss, what may I bring you?" a waiter clad in a white shirt, black slacks, and a tartan bowtie asked Denny.

She lowered her menu. "I'll try an organic tossed green salad with your house dressing on the side and your locally caught fish fillet with baked organic root vegetables."

He turned to Lydia, who tipped her head toward Denny. "I'd like the same as she ordered, please."

"I want a hamburger," Amanda told the waiter. Apparently, this was not an unusual request because the waiter made no attempt to change her mind. "And french fries," Amanda said.

"With vinegar or ketchup?" he asked.

Amanda curled her upper lip. "Ketchup."

"Sis, you amaze me." Denny spoke directly to Maureen. "You didn't see anything exotic on the menu you want to use on your TV show?"

"No." Maureen read the menu again. "Although those pan-fried scallops sound tasty."

Reality dawned. "Oh, I get it. You're writing a new cookbook. That's what this trip is all about."

Maureen flattened a linen napkin across her lap. "Denny, I might as well tell you now so you quit mentioning it. I may not be going back to the television show ever again."

"What?" Denny was floored. Her sister must be soaring upward to a spectacular new pinnacle for her to give up her lofty pedestal. "Did you get a better offer?"

"Nothing like that." Maureen selected a roll from the breadbasket. "Can't we talk about something else?"

"Are you kidding me?" Denny figured Maureen also must be suffering from jet lag.

First one tear then a stream of tears cascaded down Maureen's face. Then a river followed. She blubbered like a baby. Long, heaving sobs Denny had not seen since they were children when Maureen was manipulating their parents. Not even at the funeral did Maureen shed one tear. Whereas Denny had cried and cried.

Amanda said, "Mommy, stop crying. Everyone is staring at us."

"May I be of assistance?" Lydia asked, handing Maureen a napkin.

"I'm fine." Maureen's strangled voice betrayed her tortured emotions.

"Okay, Sis, whatever you say."

36

Chapter 12

Lydia could tell that Maureen was anything but fine. Yet the woman was her employer and Lydia had no business delving into her personal affairs. If anything, Lydia would like to cry herself, but she did her best to appear poised. She knew all too well what it was like to wear a fake mask of happiness when in truth she felt miserable inside. Not that it wasn't her own fault. Her parents' hearts would be broken if they knew of her plans to leave the church. Even her boyfriend, Jonathan, knew nothing of it. He would have tried to talk her out of leaving with Maureen Cook to come here. As far as he knew, Lydia was busy taking care of Amanda in New Jersey. Which reminded her, she had promised to write him a letter and had yet to send even a postcard. She was hoping that if she just disappeared into thin air, he would get the picture. She didn't think she loved him anymore nor did she wish to marry him and live the Amish life. She had bigger plans for herself. Of getting her GED and then attending college and studying to be a teacher.

What was she talking about? She could not afford college tuition and probably wasn't smart enough to attend one. And she could be thrown in jail at any moment. She had stolen every piece of clothing that she was wearing. Even her shoes.

Ach, what had she been thinking? She'd been caught mid-theft. Only the one time. She should have been patient and waited for her first paycheck. Greediness had seized her as if Satan himself had made her do it. And the owner of the shop had blackmailed her ever since. "Or you could step into the backroom with me," the owner, a lustful fifty-year-old man, had suggested. He'd leered at her in a way that said it all. A disgusting thought as far as Lydia was concerned. He had threatened to report her shoplifting to the police and press charges if she didn't pay a monthly fee. These would be the most expensive shoes she'd ever bought. If she could reverse the hands of time, she would have never stolen them. But she'd found that's not how life worked. How would she ever break free of the cycle?

She figured Denny might understand her predicament. But not Maureen, her employer, the woman who paid her good money that kept her out of jail.

A thought spread its wings in her mind. Lydia was tempted to stay in Scotland if they'd have her. She might never go home. She might land a job in this very hotel. Or marry someone cute. Like Alec, if he found her attractive.

Chapter 13

What on earth? was all Denny could think. She had never seen her older sister come unglued like this. Over the years, Denny had cried herself to sleep many times in the privacy of her apartment or when walking up and down the aisles of her bookstore at closing. After the death of her parents, she'd cried more times than she could calculate.

"Sis, everything all right?" Denny knew she was asking a stupid question because obviously everything was not all right. She bet James, who was handsome in his own way—tall and dark, had enjoyed several affairs. Did he want a divorce? Had Maureen caught him in the act? Not that Maureen would tell Denny the truth. She had divulged only half-truths since they were kids. "Sis?" Denny reached over and touched Maureen's soft shoulder, startling her. She flinched and then sat up straight.

Maureen reached into a pocket for a Kleenex to dab her nose. "Nothing, I'm perfectly peachy."

"Whatever." Denny didn't buy Maureen's explanation for a minute. But no use asking her about it now. Later, when the two of them were alone together, Denny would console her. Maybe Maureen was finally grieving for their parents, a heartache they could share that might bring them closer. Nah, it would never work. Maureen would clamp her lips together like a clothespin and then give Denny the cold shoulder if she mentioned their demise.

Denny admonished herself to stop thinking about them. Wasn't she going to pretend she was not grief stricken for the whole trip? Not an easy task when she was so exhausted. When trying to drift off into slumber, her mind spun like an endless loop. Another zombie night lay ahead. Denny went to a sleep disorder doctor, but he did little to help her as far as she could tell. She didn't want to take antidepressants. She had given them a couple of weeks without result. She'd even spent the night in the sleep disorder lab which she called the "night of the living dead," after an oldie scary movie. How could she sleep with people watching and monitoring her? When the ordeal was over, she couldn't wait to be set free and told that she did not have sleep apnea, which the doctor pretty much suspected. Still, he recommended she try several sleep medications, which worked fine for a week or two. But after that they lost their effectiveness. She was now resigned to a life of insomnia. Or maybe this trip would turn her sleepless nights around.

"Maureen, whatever the problem is, it's going to get better." As Denny tried to comfort her, she couldn't believe that in some ways she and Maureen had switched places. Denny hated it when her older sister spouted platitudes like this. How on earth would Denny know things were going to get better? As far as she could tell, they wouldn't.

Chapter 14

Maureen could not believe that she'd just melted into a puddle of tears in front of an audience at supper. And now she had a case of the hiccups like a frog.

At home she usually stood in the bathroom with the door closed and the water running to cry so no one would see or hear her. She would die if her younger sister knew all her weaknesses. And she had this itchy feeling someone was out to get her. She could come up with no other reason that would cause people to get sick on her TV show. Someone could have poisoned the food. At least nobody had died. What a ghastly thought. She knew the network and advertisers would drop her show for sure. They wanted no part of a scandal.

She gathered her napkin and dabbed under her eyes, which must be swollen and red. She was glad no one in the hotel had recognized her.

Several minutes later, a waitress arrived with their food.

Amanda's hand reached out to pour ketchup onto her plate. "Yummy." Her hand dove into the fries. She dragged one into the pool of ketchup, shoved it into her mouth, and chomped and then ate another. "Their ketchup tastes weird."

A few minutes later, a man wearing a cheap sports jacket strode to their table carrying a camera and took her picture. "I thought that was you," he said. "What brings you to the Isle of Skye, Mrs. Cook? Gathering recipes for Scottish delicacies?"

Maureen decided to play dumb. Which was what she felt like right now. "You must have me mixed up with someone else. Hick." She covered her mouth, then hiccupped again.

"I don't think so." He smirked. "I know who you are. This will make a great story for the *Gazette*." His smile widened, exposing buckteeth. "And maybe get picked up by the *Times* in London."

Maureen was surprised Denny didn't step in to protect her. But before she knew it, he had snapped pictures of Amanda and Lydia too. Lydia looked away but too late.

"What brings the marvelous Maureen Cook to the Isle of Skye?" he asked Maureen, who glared back at him.

"Now listen up, buddy," Denny finally said. "We will not tolerate this intrusion." She raised her hand. "Waiter, this man is bothering us."

People at nearby tables—a dozen or so—swiveled their seats to see what the commotion was all about. A waiter hustled to their table and ushered the reporter out of the dining room. The waiter came back and said, "I am so sorry, madam. If I'd known you were a celebrity, I would have seated you in the back where no one could bother you." He paused, his gaze lingering on Maureen. "Unless you like sitting where people can see you. Please do let us know your preferences."

"Too late now." Maureen shushed him away with her hands.

Amanda scowled at her mother. "You always have to be the center of attention, don't you, Mom?" Amanda said. "I hope he got a good picture of me, and that it ends up in the *New York Times*. Wouldn't that be the coolest ever?" Amanda chomped into her burger.

Maureen turned to Lydia and said, "I'm sorry you had to be bothered with this."

"It's okay." Lydia combed her fingers through her short hair. "I can't imagine people reading the paper back home at Walmart or at the donut shop would recognize me dressed this way."

Molly swooped over to the table and spoke to Maureen. "We're so very sorry you were inconvenienced."

"Not your fault." Maureen hiccupped three more times. She

only got hiccups when she was stressed. Her mind tumbled back to an embarrassing day on the set when they had to stop recording for an hour until her hiccups subsided. And then she recalled their parents' memorial service. She had been beyond stressed but had managed to hold her emotions at bay. No use crying when Denny was sobbing enough for two. In truth Maureen had been devastated, in a pit from which she might never emerge.

"I don't feel so good, Mommy." Fries filled Amanda's mouth. "My stomach."

Maureen wrapped her arm around her daughter's shoulder. "Darling, will you be okay?" Maureen was relieved to focus her attention on Amanda.

Amanda swallowed her mouthful. "I'm going to barf."

"No, you're not, sweetie," Denny said. "Probably just gobbling down your fries too fast on an empty stomach."

"Easy for you to say." Maureen never appreciated her sister's butting in. "Since when do you know so much? She might've eaten something bad at the airport." Maureen was inundated with anxiety. Had someone followed her here and poisoned the food? Was someone trying to harm her daughter and ruin her career or was she turning paranoid as Denny would say. Maureen assured herself that the television network carried insurance but her daughter—drama queen though she might be— was her number one concern. No amount of money could cover that loss should it occur.

She remembered the chilling call from the police telling her that her parents might have died in a car accident. Could she, please, come and identify the bodies and collect their belongings? "There must be some mistake" was all she could say. In a panic, she'd tried to reach James, but he didn't answer his phone. Nor did he return her texts.

In the end, brave Denny drove to the coroner's office to identify them and pick up their personal affects—rings, watches, jewelry. Maureen couldn't bear to go. Denny would probably never let her forget her cowardice.

After they'd finished their meal, a waitress spoke to the table at large. "May I serve you dessert?"

"Maybe we all need to turn in," Maureen said. "I don't want to expand into a blimp on this trip." She'd practically starved herself this last month in a fruitless effort to lose ten pounds but wouldn't mention that fact to Denny, who continued to be slim no matter what she ate. Of course, Denny ran for thirty minutes every morning and went to a gym while Maureen led a sedentary life in comparison.

"I'll have a crème Brulé, please," Denny said.

"I'm sorry, but we don't serve that." The waitress handed her a small menu. "Perhaps you'll find something in here."

Denny perused the menu. "Okay, I'll try the sticky toffee pudding. The description sounds delish." She turned to Maureen and said, "When in Rome, right?"

Amanda's face twisted as if she were in agony. "I'm not in Rome, and I want an ice cream sundae."

"Vanilla ice cream with chocolate sauce?" The waitress sent her a grin. "We can fix that for you right away." She removed Amanda's dirty plate.

"Wait just a minute, young lady," Maureen said to Amanda. "I thought you were sick."

"I changed my mind." She spoked to the waitress. "With whipped cream and a few maraschino cherries on top."

"Certainly, miss." She turned her attention to Maureen. "Anything for you, madame?"

Much as Maureen longed for something sweet, she wagged her head. "I'd better not."

Chapter 15

"And what may I bring you?" a waiter asked Lydia, who checked Maureen's expression to see if she had permission to order dessert. How could she order it when her employer was passing it up?

Maureen nodded as if reading Lydia's question from her expression. "Go ahead and eat the dessert that I'm passing up."

As Lydia perused the dessert menu, she recalled all the delicious desserts her *mam* prepared pies of every sort, puddings, and cakes. Her mouth watered at the thought of tasting them. But she would step outside her comfort zone and try something new. "The sticky toffee pudding for me too, please." Lydia was determined to be adventuresome and stretch her palate while here. If she didn't like it, she would finish it anyway. In her parents' home, she was taught to waste nothing. She wondered if the food thrown away here was given to a pig farmer. On her parents' farm, the pigs benefited from table scraps.

"I'll be right back with your dessert orders." The waiter departed into the kitchen.

As she waited, Lydia scanned the lavish dining room with its two dozen tables and was surprised to see only a few filled. Alec was apparently correct when he said the bus accident on the bridge was stopping traffic. She chuckled to herself. That tippy little ferry boat had brought them to the shore safely. She wished her friends and family could see her now. No, she didn't wish that at all. If anything, she wanted to hide. No need to worry about any of them finding her here.

She reminded herself that she wasn't the first girl in her church district to jump the fence, but she was the first in her family. When her parents found out, they would be disappointed and embarrassed. Part of the reason her father was chosen by lot to become a minister was that he was an upstanding member of the community, and his family was trustworthy. Not that God in heaven didn't do the choosing.

Chapter 16

Half an hour later Denny, her stomach full, grasped the banister and trudged up the carpeted staircase behind Maureen, Amanda, and Lydia to their rooms. After the long day, each step seemed like an ordeal. She wished she was home in her cramped little apartment in New Jersey.

Amanda tugged Lydia's hand. "I'll go to bed only if Lydia tucks me in."

Denny knew her niece's histrionics. She would try anything to get her way and was usually successful.

"Nighty-night," Denny said, but Amanda kept walking. Had Amanda outgrown her need for her Aunt Denny? Feeling downhearted, she opened her room's door. Lydia leaned inside to toss her handbag on a chair, then spun away and followed after Amanda. The flap of Lydia's bag opened. Denny couldn't help but notice something shiny and silver. With the door shut again, Denny snooped in Lydia's purse and found an ornate spoon handle. Lydia had stolen a spoon from the restaurant? Weird. From what Denny had heard, she couldn't envision an Amish woman stealing anything. Ever.

Denny wondered if she should tell Maureen but decided against it. Denny would confront Lydia when she returned. An encounter she dreaded. I mean since when had Denny turned so capital P perfect? She knew she wasn't, or she wouldn't have been searching in Lydia's bag without her consent.

Her hand rested against a silky fabric. She pulled one end and extracted a Hermès scarf. What on earth? Where would

Lydia obtain a designer brand scarf? Maybe Maureen was lending it to her. Denny's sister had more clothes than she knew what to do with. Her favorite pastime was shopping for expensive clothes, but she never had lent anything to Denny. In all fairness, Denny would have said, "No thanks."

Her mind retreated to Alec. She wondered where he lived. Alone? She wished she'd asked him straight out. She was usually bold enough to ask anyone about anything. Tomorrow she would.

Someone knocked on the door. Denny shoved the scarf and spoon back into Lydia's handbag and leaped to her feet as the door opened.

"Sorry to bother you. May I turn down the beds?" A young woman wearing a kilt and carrying two small boxes breezed into the room. "Chocolates." The woman grinned.

"Sure, okay." Denny watched her fluff the pillows, fold down the quilts with precision, and set the chocolates on each bed table. Denny longed to dive into bed after sampling a chocolate, her favorite candy.

"Anything else I can do for you?" The young woman moved toward the door.

"You can tell me what tartan you're wearing."

"Why, Clan MacDonald."

"Yes, of course." Denny decided to take advantage of the situation. "So, what's the story behind the Campbells and MacDonald feud?"

"Have you never heard of Glencoe? How the Campbells murdered the MacDonalds in their sleep?"

Denny cringed. "Oh, how terrible."

"I'm sorry, I shouldn't have told you."

"That's okay; I asked." Denny wished she hadn't. She was sick of knowing the truth.

"That was many, many years ago. In 1692." The young woman backed out into the hallway and shut the door. Minutes later it opened again, and Lydia minced in. Her vision landed on her purse as if she knew someone had been rifling through it, but she pressed her lips together. Denny was too exhausted to confront Lydia. And what good would it do? Lydia obviously had a problem. Everyone did.

To Denny's surprise, Lydia emptied her purse onto the bed in one swift motion. A myriad of items cascaded out, including a watch Denny had seen Maureen wear—or one just like it—gold loop earrings, the spoon from the dining room, the scarf, and other items.

"A spoon?" Denny was flabbergasted. "You stole a spoon from the restaurant downstairs?"

"No—I never would," Lydia sputtered. "I asked if I could bring it to our room, and the waitress said yes."

"What for? Why would you need a spoon?"

"Molly said I could have a dish of ice cream in our room later—on the house. I particularly liked this spoon." She glanced at the ornate carpet. "I wasn't going to take it home with me." Denny could buy her explanation halfway, and yet that did not explain the scarf and the earrings.

Denny knew she needed to tread carefully for fear that Lydia would quit her job and leave Maureen in the lurch. Not that Maureen couldn't take care of her own daughter. Maureen lacked confidence is all.

Lydia peered out the window. "Ach, it's snowing."

Denny strode to the window to watch a curtain of lazy snowflakes dropping to the earth. White blobs of beauty. A child at heart, Denny forgot about the spoon and the scarf.

Rapping on the door caught their attention. "Coming." Denny cracked the door. It swung open with such force that it rattled on its hinges.

"Aunt Denny, Lydia, it's snowing!" Amanda's exuberant voice revealed her excitement. "I want to go outside." She wore her hooded jacket. "Mommy won't come with me, but she said I can't go alone."

The lights flickered, then dimmed and went out.

"Oh great. I wanted to read in bed." Denny had brought

along a copy of *44 Scotland Street*, an Alexander McCall novel that took place in Edinburgh she'd spied in the bookshop. "But sure, I'll go with you." In her mind she sang "Winter Wonderland" like a ninny. Hadn't she complained about the snow this past winter? Not that it didn't sometimes snow well into spring in New Jersey. She was glad for the light produced by her iPhone's flashlight.

"You coming?" she asked Lydia.

"Yah, sure. Give me a minute to find my coat and hat." Lydia sounded as enthusiastic as Amanda.

Denny's arms wrestled themselves into her jacket and gloves, then she plopped her hat atop her head. She was surprised when she found Maureen in the hall looking for them. "You want to come down with us?" Denny asked her.

"I guess. I'll sit inside somewhere and have tea and that dessert I missed." Maureen patted her tummy. "Not that I should be eating more sweets."

When Denny descended the stairs, she walked right into Alec. "What are you doing here?" she asked.

He laughed. "I hope you're not disappointed." His wide grin was illuminated by candles on the front desk. "When I heard the weather report, I asked if I could use the spare bedroom in the basement here in case it snowed and my car got stuck."

Denny realized she was gaping up at him. "The more the merrier." She admonished herself for acting so eager to spend time with him. For all she knew, he wanted to be with Lydia or Molly. "Won't your wife be expecting you?" Denny asked.

He tilted his head. "Are you asking me if I'm married?"

Denny felt like a goof but too late now. "I guess so. Well, are you?"

"No wife at home waiting for me," he said. "Not yet."

Which meant what? Denny asked herself. "You're engaged?"

"No." Although it was difficult to see his features in the darkness, his mouth seemed to widen into a grin. "And since you are being so brash, may I ask you if you have a young man waiting for you back in the States?"

"Not at the moment." She didn't want him to think that she rarely dated. "Care to join us outside?"

"Absolutely." Alec grabbed his jacket off the coatrack, searched the pockets, then pulled on his cap and gloves.

As they exited the hotel, Denny felt cold air surround her and saw a cloudy puff float from Alec's mouth, telling her that the temperature plunged.

A swirl of activity awaited them. Several families with children left the hotel yelling and shouting. Most of the adults wore laughing faces—along with several who were dour as they leapt into their cars and sped away.

Denny looked up as the snow increased. "When it snows on Skye, it doesn't mess around." She felt an icy missile hit the side of her head. "Hey, who threw that?" Then she heard Amanda's peel of laughter and realized the girl had lobbed a snowball at her.

"Why you little…" Denny's hand raised to her mouth while she restrained herself from spewing out a swear word she hadn't thought of since her teenage years that she figured Alec would disapprove of. And anyway, wasn't she trying to improve her life rather than debase it?

Denny gathered up a handful of snow, packed it together into an orb, and threw it at Amanda, hitting her in the shoulder. Before long a dozen people of all ages were partaking in their snowball fight. Even Alec, who fortunately was on Denny's team.

"Hey, Jack." Alec hurled a snowball at a man whom he apparently knew.

"Watch it, laddie." The man gathered snow and threw a snowball at Alec, hitting him in the chest.

"You started it," the man said.

"Aye, and I call for a truce."

"Be on my side," Amanda yelled to Lydia, who hurled a snowball at Denny with force. Denny did not appreciate Lydia's zeal and wondered if the girl had purposely tried to hurt her.

51

"Where did you learn to throw like that?" Alec asked Lydia, who gathered snow into another ball and tossed it at Alec, hitting him in the chest.

"I played baseball with my brothers." Lydia bent to gather more snow.

Denny saw that Lydia had garnered Alec's full attention. He fashioned more snow into a ball and threw it at Lydia with little force. He apparently did not want to harm her.

Lydia threw her head back and laughed. "Is that the best you can do?"

Through a window, Denny noticed Maureen inside watching them the way their mother would have. A spectator. Maureen even looked like Mom, the way she massaged her hands together. Dad would have joined in the fun. Denny missed them both, but she missed Dad the most. Would Denny always be a child seeking her parents' approval?

Chapter 17

A tangle of emotions knotted through Maureen's brain as she watched the snowball fight gather momentum. Nimble Denny had always been good at sports, but Maureen threw like a girl. She cringed as she recalled her high school PE classes. She'd hidden in the safety of the locker room when the other girls flocked onto the softball field with glee. Thankfully, her physical education teacher had let her slide. Maureen's forte had shone in her cooking classes. At home, she'd helped her mother's housekeeper prepare meals and had soon surpassed the woman's talents. Maureen recorded Martha Stewart and all the best cooking shows to watch after her homework was done. She was practically a straight A student, so her parents did not complain. And sometimes they would watch the cooking shows with her while athletic Denny practiced shooting hoops on the basketball court outside of the kitchen.

When it came time to attend college, she chose to major in home economics, which her father thought was a waste of time. "Why spend my money learning about things you already know how to do?" he'd asked, his voice full of laughter that disclosed his lack of pride. Denny had always been the clever one, even though her grades did not reveal it. Her father admired Denny's pluckiness. She was the only one in the family who would stand up to him, which he found admirable.

But Maureen was not a complete flop, not that her father would ever admit it. Only mom had encouraged her with her cooking. Maureen smiled as her culinary fame replayed itself in her mind. But she was about to lose it all. Her smile flattened and her face sagged. Without her cooking show, she would be a nobody again. No respect from anyone. Invisible.

She remembered meeting James at a college dance and becoming infatuated with him the moment he had spoken. She'd had a boyfriend, but she gladly dropped him when she met James. Rusty, with his splash of freckles, had been such a nice guy and had treated her like royalty, but Maureen had preferred James's style, much like her own father's. She wondered if she would have been attracted to him if she'd met him today. She might have not married James and been happily wedded to Rusty. But then she wouldn't have her daughter—their daughter, that is. There was no way to win; she would never admit that James was not Amanda's real father. As long as Amanda never took a genealogy test, no one would ever know that Rusty was her biological father. A secret Maureen would take to her grave. She recalled revealing to James that she was pregnant. He had been stunned, then ecstatic, thankfully, and had suggested they get married right away. Maureen's parents had been over the moon. As if poised for this moment, Mom started planning the wedding immediately. A list of caterers owed Maureen's mother their allegiance. A huge sit-down affair for four hundred mentioned in the *New York Times*. What could be better?

Chapter 18

Lydia was delighted she could throw a ball as well as her brothers. Thrilled to have garnered Alec's attention. And yet she felt a pang of regret for leaving her brothers and her little sister, not to mention her parents. And Jonathan. Not that she wouldn't be expected to get married, bear children, and then stay home to care for them. Wait a minute. Didn't she want a family and children? Yes, eventually. But not yet.

A snowball flew past her like a missile. Her head snapped around to see Alec, as handsome as can be and laughing. She recalled Jonathan had always been the object of her desires. She'd known him since she was a little girl and had decided they would get married at the age of six. She'd even chosen the sky-blue fabric that matched her eyes for her wedding dress. She'd never wavered from her love for him until she'd taken her job in New Jersey caring for Amanda. Maureen had opened a new world for her like Pandora's tantalizing box. She'd even taken her to get a driver's license, meaning Lydia had to submit to having her picture taken. As well as a photo for a passport. If her father could see those photos, he would lose all respect for her. Her mam might not care as much. What was Lydia thinking? Her mother would be heartbroken.

Two of her brothers who had not yet been baptized had purchased a junker and had hidden it, but she figured her parents knew where the old car was stashed and turned a blind eye. But Dat had called Lydia the apple of his eye, meaning he was extremely fond and proud of her. To lose that esteem would be like losing her life. And yet that's most likely what would happen when he found out she might leave the church. Not that she had been baptized yet. Thankfully. She'd put that lifetime commitment off, even though she'd told Jonathan she was planning to take the necessary baptismal classes.

She scanned the area around her and noticed that most of the people were headed toward the hotel again or climbing into their cars. Falling in with them, she found both guests and employees speaking at once and laughing. She didn't recognize some of the languages. French, Portuguese, Italian? No one speaking Pennsylvania Dutch or German.

As she made her way to the hotel, Alec strolled alongside her. She longed to take his hand for stability but knew that would be wrong. As she considered this, her feet flew out in front of her, and she fell on her rear end in a most unladylike fashion.

"Whoops." Alec helped her to her feet. The snow had turned into a white blanket of smaller particles. The ground was covered. These are the winters she had grown up with in Lancaster County, so she figured she could navigate her way. But when Alec offered her his elbow, she took it.

He said, "You have quite a pitching arm."

"I'm sorry if I hurt you."

"You wounded only my pride." He massaged his cheek.

"Everyone, look." Amanda dropped to the ground. "I can make a snow angel."

"Wonderful, but it's time to go inside." Lydia knew how headstrong Amanda was but would not be sidetracked.

"But I want to stay outside and play all night."

"Your mother would not approve of you being out here by yourself."

Amanda finally stood, and Lydia brushed the snow off Amanda's hair and jacket. At Amanda's age, Lydia would've done exactly the same thing. Life was so much simpler and carefree when Lydia was a girl.

As they entered the hotel's front doors and stepped inside the foyer, candlelight cast dancing shadows, reminding Lydia of home. Never living with electricity, she would not miss it in the slightest. She grinned at her advantage, and yet she had adapted to Maureen's way of life. She reveled in it. She was as bad as Amanda when it came to watching TV. Some nights she'd stay up late to watch some silly show and fall asleep on the couch and yawn the whole next day.

Inside the front door, hotel guests stomped snow off their shoes and shed their jackets and coats while employees took and shook them. A man stoked the fire in the hearth, and people gravitated to it for warmth.

A clump of employees gathered around an older woman dressed in a kilt and a white blouse with a ruffle in the front, who was apparently in charge.

"How can we work in the darkness, and how can we prepare the next meal without electricity?" a young Scottish woman asked.

"Has anyone tried to start up the generator?" The older woman clasped her ample hips.

"Yes. Two of the men tried without success."

"Thank the dear Lord, we have gas stoves for cooking," one young woman said. "But will the morning crew be able to come to work tomorrow with all the snow?"

Lydia saw little problem. She moved over and spoke to the older woman. "I'm used to cooking on gas stoves. I could assist you with breakfast."

"Looks like we could use the help," the woman said. Lydia saw all eyes turning in her direction. "If you're sure."

Maureen strode forward. "This young woman works for me. Is there a problem?"

"I'm the night manager, Mrs. Ross." The older woman, who must be Mam's age, rubbed her hands together. "As you can see, our power is out. We usually serve hot chocolate and cookies in the evening and a full breakfast in the morning." She looked distressed; the corners of her mouth pulled back. "And we can't get the generator working." She smiled at Lydia. "But good news. This young lady has offered to help."

Maureen's sculpted brows lowered. "I bet I can cook better than Lydia. Well, I know I can. I'm a professional chef."

"But you came to us so that we could serve you not the other way around."

"This will be fun for me, I assure you." Maureen crossed her arms. "Better than sitting around feeling sorry for myself."

Lydia couldn't imagine why Maureen would feel sorry for herself, but she had come to understand that the *Englisch* life was still foreign to her.

When Lydia glanced over to the front door, she saw Denny and Alec chatting, their heads close together as if they were having a private conversation. Denny fluffed her hair and looked up to him with a flirtatious expression on her face. Lydia wished she were a fly on the wall so that she could overhear.

"How about hot chocolate?" Maureen's voice bubbled with exuberance. "I have my own special recipe if you have marshmallows and whole cream. And if someone fetches me a bowl, I can whip up some of my award-winning snickerdoodle cookies. Doesn't that sound yummy?"

"Yes, madam." Alec's laughter filled the room.

Lydia couldn't help but admire Maureen's outgoing personality. Her success. Why, Lydia wouldn't think of speaking up like that. She was a nobody again. An assistant was what she would be for the rest of her life.

Chapter 19

No doubt about it, Denny noticed Alec glancing at Lydia even when speaking to Denny. How rude. Yet what man wouldn't be attracted to Lydia's wholesome good looks and athletic abilities? She had made slipping on her rear end appear graceful. And she seemed to always be in a cheerful mood.

Denny decided to be more amiable the rest of the trip and not let anything prod her into a funk. Spending so much time with her marvelous, can-do-anything older sister was probably the root of Denny's snarly mood.

In truth, they were in the same rowboat when it came to losing their parents.

As Denny struggled out of her jacket, she remembered how she'd watched an old detective show—a British murder mystery—the night before she'd left for this trip. She was traveling to Scotland but couldn't find a Scottish show. But Scotland was part of the British Isles, she'd told herself.

Later when getting ready for bed, Denny had contemplated the fact that her parents could have been targeted, just like the man in the TV show. Their father was a big-shot Wall Street trader, but his death had not even been mentioned by the *New York Times*. Not that she wanted her parents' personal lives to be dragged through the mud. But how is it that they died penniless? Worse than penniless. In debt. What was that all about?

Denny knew she should be grateful her sister was such a success, but Maureen's achievements seemed to detract from Denny's, making her shrink.

How would Denny cope without her parents' support? She'd hoped to borrow money from them to buy more inventory for her bookstore. Unless Maureen and James saved the day. The thought of begging for their help made Denny wince. Maybe death would be the easiest escape.

But dread filled her at the thought. If she had cancer, she would fight it with all her might.

Out of the corner of her eye, she saw movement. A rat? Panic seized her. Before she could stop herself, she blurted out a pitiful scream.

"What's wrong?" Alec moved closer.

"I saw something." Denny imagined a rodent running up her leg, and she shivered at the thought. "A mouse or a rat." They scared Denny down to her bones.

Lydia chortled. "A tiny little mouse won't hurt you."

Denny was embarrassed by her reaction, but how dare Lydia laugh at her? Denny aimed her flashlight under the furniture but saw nothing.

"Princess usually dispatches with any vermin swifter than any cat." Mrs. Ross spoke in Denny's ear. "Sorry you were frightened."

"I wasn't afraid but rather surprised." Denny would never admit her many phobias. She could bluff her way through anything. So far.

Chapter 20

Back in the driver's seat, Maureen thought with a burst of confidence. She could handle anything that came her way, even if she did lose her job. So what? She was still the Marvelous Maureen Cook.

"Show me what's in the refrigerator." She put out a hand to steady herself. Hard to believe they functioned in such a small space with such outdated equipment, but Maureen would keep her thoughts to herself. "Are any of the cooks still here?"

Mrs. Ross handed her a flashlight with a stronger beam. "No, our evening cook's shift just ended. She asked if she could go home when the snow started, and I said yes, so she left."

"No matter," Maureen said. "I can handle everything with Lydia's help." Maureen opened the mammoth refrigerator door. She canvassed the contents and was glad to see all that she'd need. Without electricity, cold ingredients would need to be used in the morning anyway. She gathered up cream, milk, and eggs. Then she shut the door quickly using her hip.

Denny meandered into the kitchen and watched her.

Maureen was grateful for the flashlight but it flickered. She was afraid the battery was on its last leg. "Denny, get over here." The flashlight's beam illuminated the knobs on the front of the stove. "I need your help."

"Me? You know I'm a lost cause in the kitchen."

Maureen's heart beat faster. At home on her TV show, she always had an assistant setting out all the ingredients ahead of time. She had never felt under pressure like this. She tried to calm her racing mind without success. In spite of the chilly air, she felt dampness gathering under her armpits. Then she smelled smoke.

"What's happening? My cookies aren't even in the oven yet."

She cracked the oven door, and a billow of heat and smoke belched out. Someone had left food from dinner in the oven—what appeared to be a pie. She coughed. Her eyes burned. The smoke detector began to screech.

"What's happening?" Mrs. Ross dashed into the room.

Maureen was glad to see no flames. She assured herself the whole kitchen wasn't on fire. But how could she turn off the smoke detector?

"What's happening?" Mrs. Ross asked again over the blaring noise.

Maureen yelled to be heard over the smoke detector. "I guess I turned the oven on too high, and there was something in it already. A cook left what appears to be a pie in the oven."

"She probably meant to keep it warm in case anyone wanted more dessert." Mrs. Ross's words were barely audible.

Denny dashed into the kitchen with Alec and Molly. "Everything okay, Sis?" Denny asked.

"Are you kidding?" Maureen marveled at the stupid question, because obviously everything was not all right.

"What on earth is the problem?" Denny shouted.

"Would someone please turn off that incessant smoke detector?" Maureen felt a meltdown approaching. She'd always kept her cool when on live TV. Except that last show.

Mrs. Ross pointed up to the ceiling. "It's too high for me. Someone will have to fetch a ladder."

"Tell me where it is, and I'll get it," Alec said.

Mrs. Ross spoke into Alec's ear. He stepped out of the kitchen and came back a moment later carrying a ladder. He pulled it open and climbed to the top, then extracted the battery from the smoke detector. The silence was a balm to Maureen's ears, but smoke filled the air. Several more smoke detectors blared out their warnings, and hotel guests scrambled down the staircase to see if they needed to evacuate the building.

"No," Alec told them. "Just smoke from the kitchen setting off the alarms."

"Sorry for the inconvenience," Molly said to a woman clad in her bathrobe.

"At least our sprinkler system didn't go off." Mrs. Ross opened the back door. "We would have had to close the whole hotel. Nothing to be done about the smoke without a fan running, except open the door and windows to let fresh air in." Mrs. Ross opened a window above the sink.

"I am so sorry." Maureen coughed. "Are you keeping an eye on the hot chocolate?" she asked Lydia.

"Yah, you can count on me." Lydia continued to stir the chocolaty concoction.

Mrs. Ross switched off the stove and then patted Lydia's shoulder. "You're an angel." Mrs. Ross brought out ceramic mugs. "We have tins of shortbread to serve with it." She turned to Maureen and said, "Please, no more cooking."

"Okay." Maureen was baffled that she hadn't thought to turn off the oven. What was wrong with her? She felt deflated, like a balloon losing its air. She could barely breathe with all the smoke. At least no one at home could see her debacle. She was beyond belief humiliated.

"Don't just stand there, Sis." Denny stuffed her hands into hot mitts, lifted the smoking pie out of the oven, and dumped it in the sink, then she turned on the water taps and flushed water over it, producing a cloud of sizzling smoky steam.

Why hadn't Maureen thought to do that? She was used to being in command. On top of the world. The Marvelous Mrs. Cook.

Smoke detectors blared throughout the hotel as a sooty cloud floated into the dining room and triggered the whole system. An older couple dressed in bathrobes trotted downstairs. Mrs. Ross assured them that everything was alright. She apologized profusely when in fact Maureen was the source of the problem. Well, not the electrical outage. How on earth would they make it through the night?

Several people said they were checking out and moving to another hotel before the snow got much deeper. Not that Maureen blamed them. She considered doing the same thing but figured it was impossible.

Fatigue encompassed her. She longed to crawl into bed and snuggle under the covers and read. She'd brought a book but was too tired to even change into her pajamas. And how would she see the words on the pages?

Chapter 21

Lydia was fascinated to see Maureen the cause of such a chaotic calamity. Lydia had always pictured her employer as calm and in control in all circumstances. But not so. Lydia must not be judgmental, but she would have checked in the oven first. Didn't everyone know to crack the oven door? She thought of how proficient her mam was in the kitchen. Mam was always the first one up and had coffee and food ready for Dat and the family when they arose.

Lydia admonished herself to stay focused and not burn the hot chocolate. Growing up with no electricity, she'd learned to use all her senses. This kitchen was dark, but she would keep centered on her task. She was used to living with only flashlights, propane lighting, or candles illuminating their home, and natural gas or wood heating. She was not afraid of the cold. Their house had no central heating, which encouraged all family members to gather around the fireplace and kitchen. Not the television set, the way she had since moving into the Cooks' house.

Ach, she'd wasted so many hours watching TV while the laundry washed and dried when she could have been doing something productive. She was glad her parents couldn't see her lazing around with her feet up all day, accomplishing nothing and staying up too late. At home on the farm, she would have gathered eggs before breakfast and then helped her mam serve the food to the rest of the family. After, she would have washed dishes and the pots and pans. Then she'd helped her mam clean the kitchen until it sparkled. She had to admit she liked Maureen's dishwasher. But washing the dishes with her mam at her side had brought her comfort and a feeling of community, knowing that all the other Amish women in the district were also washing dishes.

Inhaling the aroma of the warming hot milk, she continued to stir in methodical motions until she felt heat radiating from her brew, telling her the hot chocolate was warm enough to serve.

"Do you have marshmallows?" she asked, hoping a member of the hotel's staff was standing nearby.

"Yes," Molly answered. "Large or little?"

"Any size will do."

"Coming right up." Molly shined her flashlight across the room, then came back and stood at Lydia's side. "I brought you wee marshmallows—the little ones."

"Perfect."

"Is there enough hot chocolate for me to have a cup?"

"Yah, I doubt many people will want any." Lydia was flattered that Molly would want to taste her hot chocolate.

"A mass exodus," Molly said. "I doubt if all but Alec, your entourage, and the honeymooners haven't left."

Chapter 22

Denny was flabbergasted that her sister would be such a doofus. Wasn't she a professional chef? Wasn't she the older sister who always came out victorious?

A member of the staff, a young woman clad in a kilt, bustled up to them. "Princess is having her pups."

"Oh no, it's too cold." Denny said.

"I can assist." Lydia stepped forward. "On the farm, I've helped many animals give birth."

"That would be wonderful," Molly said. "She's in the basement."

"In my room?" Alec asked.

"No, but close by."

They descended the stairs. Ahead tall shelves supporting canned goods and bottled drinks lined the walls.

Denny trailed the group and rubbed her arms for warmth. "I can help too." She wouldn't let Lydia outdo her. And she was curious to see Alec's room. But when they reached the soon-to-be-mother, they found that Princess was just nesting, according to Lydia.

"A common occurrence," Lydia said. "She might nest for days. Animals often do."

Flashlight in hand, Denny glanced into Alec's bedroom. A single bed, a nightstand with a nonworking lamp. A weighty book by the bed. She wondered what he was reading but decided to not venture into the room to see.

"She's preparing a place to give birth, but she's not ready," Lydia said.

Denny saw the dog curled on the floor on a blanket that must be her bed.

"I can hardly wait." Lydia's voice was giddy.

Exactly what Denny was thinking but didn't want to seem overly enthusiastic. She hated waiting and had always been impatient. Denny knew this fact about herself, but so what? There were worse traits, such as laziness.

Alec said, "I'll make her a whelping box out of scraps of wood that's stored in one of the sheds out back and line it with newspaper."

"You'd do that?" Denny's admiration for him blossomed.

"Aye, I love animals. Especially dogs."

"I do too. And reading."

He nodded. "Nothing better than a good book."

Denny pondered what else they had in common. Her mind spun back to her bookstore. While here she'd intended to purchase books. But the snow would make that chore impossible for at least a day. In the morning, she might walk into Portree and see what she could find. She bet she would discover most of the stores empty. Maybe not even open.

"Good night," she said to Alec. She hated to leave him of all silly things.

He nodded in her direction and said, "Hope you sleep well."

"Thanks." Denny climbed the stairs and peered out a window to see white. In the distance, she could make out a few lights, which must be Portree.

"I'm going to bed," Maureen said, startling Denny. "After my debacle, I don't dare show my face anywhere."

"No one will know," Denny said. "You're a stranger to most of the people in this hotel."

"What if that reporter comes back?" Maureen's face looked ghoulish in the darkness.

"No one's going anywhere in this snow." For the first time, Denny felt sorry for her superstar sister.

Amanda pressed her face against the glass window. "Can't we go outside again?"

"No." Both Denny and Maureen answered in unison.

"Where is Lydia?" Maureen asked. "She is supposed to be looking after you."

"I don't need looking after," Amanda said. "You act like I'm a little baby."

In the darkened room, Denny grinned. Couldn't Maureen take care of her own daughter? "You go upstairs with your mom," Denny said to Amanda. "Time to catch up on your sleep."

"But I want to watch TV."

"Pretty hard to do without electricity, sweetie." Denny chuckled under her breath. "Besides, I didn't see televisions in any of the rooms. Maybe they have a room downstairs with a TV."

"What kind of a dumb hotel is this anyway?" Amanda stomped her foot on the floor. "Mommy wrecked everything when she burned something in the oven."

"Hold on, your mother is not responsible for the snow or the power outage."

"Thank you for stating the obvious, Denny." Maureen's voice came out like she was defeated. "You coming upstairs?"

"Not yet." Denny decided to stay put in case Alec showed up again. She didn't trust sweet and lovely Lydia. Denny had plenty to talk about with Alec. She could turn on the charm when she needed to. She heard voices mingling. Alec and Lydia. Denny wished this didn't bother her, but it did.

The day after their parents' memorial service her former boyfriend sent her a text. A text of all puny gestures. He was sorry about the death of her parents but he didn't see a future with her. She'd needed to be held as she wept, but he was long gone. She bet he was skiing in some resort far away from her. Probably taking that trip to Switzerland he'd always talked about. Denny wondered if he'd brought along a new girlfriend but didn't have the energy to find out. What good would knowing about it do Denny now?

Several people had sent her sympathy cards, but she hadn't had the energy to read them beyond what some employee at

Hallmark had stated. Still, she appreciated the sentiment. The sender was sorry, please accept their sympathy. Just words falling to the earth in silence like shriveled leaves.

Her father had never liked Kevin, and now she wished she'd asked him why. She should have listened to Dad more. She would if he were still alive. She was sure of it. He had been dead set against her opening a bookstore. "I'm a stockbroker, a businessman," he'd told her. She took offense when she could have taken his advice. "Buy low and sell high" was one of his favorite sayings. And "it's a dog-eat-dog world."

In hindsight he could have offered her much needed information. As an English literature major in college, she knew nothing about operating a business. No wonder she was in the red; more money was going out than was coming in. One thing for sure, in order for her store to keep its doors open, she needed more inventory. Did she know so little about her customers that she'd purchased the wrong books?

She continued to gaze out at the whiteness. Talk about silent. She recalled an oldies song her mother used to play, "The Sound of Silence" by Simon and Garfunkel. Like a slap on the face, Denny was staggered by how little she'd appreciated her mother when she was alive. She could think of a thousand topics she would talk to Mom about today. They could have gone to a tea shop and sat across the table from each other. But too late now. The two of them could be on this trip together to keep Maureen company.

Denny was startled by a flash of light. She spun around and saw Alec and Lydia approaching her with a flashlight.

"I'm sorry, I didn't mean to startle you," he said to Denny. "You looked deep in thought."

"Not a problem." Denny's elbow resting in the windowsill, she tried to look nonchalant—as if she hadn't a care in the world. "I was just thinking about how beautiful and peaceful it is outside. But I guess by morning we'll be freezing."

"I'll have a look at the generator," he said. "See if I can get it working."

"Wait. Before you skedaddle, I have a few questions for you." She pivoted to Lydia and said, "I think Maureen might need you while I speak to Alec." Denny composed a serious mask of concern when all she wanted was to get rid of her and be alone with him.

As they watched Lydia leave, Denny's mind scrambled for ideas. She was pleased when one took shape in her brain. "Is there a used bookstore in the town of Portree?" she asked. "Or anywhere else nearby?"

"There's a quaint little shop in Portree, but I don't know that it sells used books."

"Any bookstore would be fine. I'm not sure what I'm looking for. Books I can't find at home."

"With all that fresh snow, I'll have to wait and see how my car drives. It's not a four-wheel-drive vehicle. I'm ill prepared. It usually only rains here."

"We could always walk."

"Aye, if Maureen and Amanda want to go with us."

"Lydia could stay here with Amanda. And Maureen doesn't much care for walking."

"We'll have to wait and see what tomorrow brings." He turned away from her and peered out the window. "The snow is coming down harder. I've never seen so much."

It occurred to Denny that Alec's mind might be grappling for excuses not to go anywhere with her ever. He may have no interest in her nor even like reading. Not everyone did, and she must not judge him lest she be judged. Where did that admonition come from? She recalled her parents forcing her and Maureen to go to Sunday school when they were young and through high school. In any case, it was the truth. It was always easier to see a speck in someone else's eye past the logjam in her own vision. She herself had sinned often. She'd lied to her parents. Pilfered from their liquor cabinet. Things so terrible she would not admit them even to herself.

Denny didn't want to be alone. But she could tell Alec was moving away from her as he rotated toward the kitchen.

71

"Hey, wait up." She placed a hand on his forearm for a moment. "Tell me more about yourself."

"What are you asking? Do you mean why do something mundane like be a hired driver?"

That was exactly what she was asking but realized the question sounded judgmental.

"You must think I'm nosy." She felt her pulse speeding up. Now what would she say? "There's nothing wrong with driving around this beautiful location."

"Truth is, I went to college, but I was expelled when I was falsely accused by a professor of cheating on a test." He cleared his throat. "I lost my scholarship as well."

Denny was dumbfounded by his honesty. Without thinking she opened her mouth and spoke. "I've cheated and lied but was never caught," she said. Something she had never admitted to anyone. Why speak to him this way? She felt exposed, even in the darkness. She wished she could hide.

She gathered herself together. "But I'm not lying about my business. I do own a thriving little bookshop." Thriving? *Floundering* would be a better description. Low on stock and customers. She couldn't compete with Amazon. But why start being honest now? When she went home, she would never see Alec again.

Her sister had excelled in all her endeavors. The magnificent Maureen with Denny struggling to keep up. Without success.

But things had been changing. Denny had been baffled when Maureen started crying at supper. And her fiasco in the kitchen? Denny had never seen Maureen make such ghastly mistakes. Denny's head spun as she tried to make sense of things. She was glad she had never told Maureen of her own terrible blunders. If and when her bookshop went under, she would have to make up some lie to cover her tracks rather than to tell Maureen about it. No use worrying about their parents' disapproval anymore. They would have been terribly disappointed in her. Not that she blamed them; she was disappointed in herself.

"I've never seen a generator before." Denny turned to Alec. "I've always wondered how they worked." Not true.

"It's in an outbuilding. I'll take you with me as long as you don't mind being cold and in the dark."

"Nah, I'm not afraid of anything." She was glad she was shrouded in darkness.

"How about an occasional mouse?"

Denny stiffened as she felt terror close in on her. Why had she made such a grandiose statement about herself when in fact she had many fears. Too many. But now was not the time to examine them.

He found another flashlight and a couple of shortbread cookies in a tin container as they passed through the kitchen. He handed them to her.

"Thanks." She bit into the cookie and savored it as the buttery flavor melted in her mouth. "Yummy." Once outside, she realized she had stopped walking.

"You coming?"

"Sorry to slow you down." What an idiot. "Yes, I'm coming."

The snow crunched under their feet. A romantic setting if ever there were one. She flicked the flashlight on and was pleased that it sent out a strong beam. "Thanks for being my knight in shining armor." A dumb statement, she thought, then wondered if he would rather have Lydia with him. But she would not offer a replacement. "Lead the way," she said, acting cavalier.

He turned back to her. "Are you sure you wouldn't rather wait in the hotel by the fire?"

"It's not exactly warm and cozy in there either. At least I'm working off a little of my dinner. And I enjoy walking."

He shrugged as if taking in her statement, then continued his trek to the shed.

The snow fell without subsiding. Denny watched puffball flakes accumulate on Alec's hat and shoulders. Except for the crunching under foot, she was struck by the silence. No tires rotating nor voices chattering. No horns honking. She felt as though they were the only two people in the world.

As they moved away from the hotel, she considered that he might rather have some local lass like Molly who was far more beautiful than Denny, who didn't consider herself beautiful at all. No matter what Mom had told her.

Denny followed Alec's light toward a low outbuilding. He kicked accumulated snow away from a door and pulled it open. He aimed his flashlight's beam toward a large contraption that must be the generator. He stepped inside the dark room and let out a groan. "No petrol," he said.

"What?" Denny didn't understand his meaning.

"Gasoline is what powers this." He picked up what must be an empty gas can, then tossed it aside. "It's so late in the year that probably no one thought to refill these. Perhaps the hotel can request gas to be delivered tomorrow morning. If the snow lets up and a truck can make it in."

In the darkness, Denny moved closer to him. She felt like dropping all pretense and draping her arms around him and kissing him. She could feel a magnetic current zinging between them. She wasn't imagining that. It was tangible. Neither said a word for several minutes, but warmth spread throughout her, making her want to shed off her jacket. And what? Have a fling with a near stranger while on holiday?

She recalled when in college going to a party and drinking too much. She had been attracted to a football player who took notice of her, then led her to a bedroom in the house and made love to her. Only there was no love on his part. Just casual sex he probably didn't even remember. He didn't call as he promised, nor did he seem to recognize her when they passed each other on campus after that quickie. She wasn't even a blip on his radar. She'd lost her virginity, something she could never regain. She had promised herself never to repeat that impetuous action again.

But here, on this chilly night surrounded by glorious snow and serenity, she might cave in and do anything Alec asked. The word *no* didn't seem to be in her vocabulary anymore.

She wondered what he was thinking. That she was just some

dumb bimbo tourist? A dime a dozen. She imagined many women had come on to this handsome Scottish man. He must be used to it, which made her resentful. She would not play easy to get. If he wanted her, she would make him work.

To break his spell, Denny yawned audibly. "I'm bushed and cold. At least they have natural gas burners on their stoves." She turned away from him and stepped toward the door. "We can heat water and make coffee and tea, can't we?"

"We? Aren't you a hotel guest? Surely someone can make that for you."

Was he referring to someone like Molly or Lydia? According to the Amish novels Denny had read, if Lydia was Amish, she could do everything without electricity.

"Not much chance of that." Denny picked up her pace.

"Lass, slow down. What's your hurry?" Alec's boots crunched in the powdery snow. "I can't keep up with you."

Denny turned around and giggled. A girlish giggle. Not her usual style. She wanted people to see her as a sophisticated lady.

Chapter 23

Maureen had been so horror stricken in the kitchen that she forgot about losing her job. Had she ever been more flustered?

"Lydia, you might as well go to bed."

"*Danke*, I think I will." Through the darkened room, Maureen watched the graceful young woman exit. The door sighed shut. Maureen figured Lydia was exhausted and didn't want to deal with Amanda any more than Maureen did. How had she managed to raise such a rebellious young woman? The whole world had tipped off its axis as far as Maureen was concerned. Few children obeyed their parents the way they did in the old days. Maureen and Denny had been good little girls for the most part. Their father demanded respect.

"Mommy, the battery in my phone is going dead. I wanna play games."

Maureen realized she didn't have the right kind of plug-ins or adapters. She assumed the hotel would provide them, but she'd forgotten to ask when they checked in. "No electricity, sweetheart."

"What will I do?"

"I could read to you."

"Some dumb book?"

"It's been my favorite ever since high school." Maureen had read and reread Daphne du Maurier's 1938 novel *Rebecca* so many times she practically knew it by heart. Yet she always enjoyed reading it much more than watching the 1940 Hitchcock movie. And she had no use for the newer 2020 version even though it was in color. She preferred black and white. Maureen was old-fashioned that way.

"Well?" Amanda said. "Okay. Go ahead and read me the first page. Maybe it will put me to sleep."

Maureen didn't need a lamp on; she'd read it so many times. "Last night I dreamt I went to Manderley again."

"Does this have a happy ending?" Amanda flopped on her side.

"Yes and no."

"Is it scary?"

"Yes and no."

"Can't you just give me a straight answer? Why do you always do this?"

"Always do what?"

"Lie to me."

Maureen was dumbfounded. She avoided lying when at all possible. Yes, she realized she had bent the truth to shield Amanda from sadness. But what good would telling Amanda about her disappointments do?

"Are you and Daddy getting a divorce or what?"

"What on earth gave you that idea?"

"He's not here, is he?" Amanda rassled in her sheets. "And you sleep in separate bedrooms."

"That's because your father has sleep apnea. I can't get a minute's sleep with his machine going on all night."

"But why didn't he come on this trip?"

"I invited him, but his work schedule is too full." Maureen's mind struggled to recall her husband's excuses. "His clients need him."

"More than you and I do? He loves them more than he loves us?"

Maureen had often wondered the same thing, but she said, "Of course not, sweetheart. He loves you more than anything."

"He sure has a strange way of showing it."

"If he didn't work, we wouldn't be able to afford this trip. Or to live in our beautiful house in a nice neighborhood. And a private school." Maureen would give all that up. Well, maybe not anymore. Not since she might get fired from her job.

"Mom, you're such a loser. You're blind to what's right in front of you."

Maureen closed her book to see if her daughter was serious. Of course, Amanda knew her grandparents had recently died, but she couldn't possibly know about her TV show catastrophe, could she?

"Hey there, I'm still your mother. Show more respect."

"Do I have to spell it out for you?" Amanda propped yourself on one elbow. "He's having an affair."

Laughter burbled out of Maureen's mouth. "He never would."

"Are you kidding me? Men are scum."

"Not your father. He'd be appalled if he could hear you."

"Mom, I overheard him telling someone named Cheryl that he loved her on his cell phone."

"You must have heard it wrong." Maureen knew there was a woman named Cheryl in James's office. A tall, beautiful brunette. Maureen simply would not believe it. Although she could envision this Cheryl woman in her stilettoes slinking around the office enticing her husband.

"Have it your way, Mommy. Just don't be surprised when the bomb lands, exploding your world into smithereens."

Just last month Maureen had felt independent and unshakable. A pillar of strength. She'd assured herself she could always move back with her parents if James left her—not that he would. Since their parents' demise, she and Denny had listed their home, only to find their parents had taken out a second mortgage they'd neglected to mention to either Maureen or Denny.

Since their deaths, as well as the problems at work, she'd used shopping as a soothing mechanism. Her charge card was accumulating debt faster than she could pay it off, a fact that she had not mentioned to James. If he only knew how expensive this trip was, he would be furious. She dreaded the confrontation.

Chapter 24

Lydia was used to moving around in semidarkness after sunset and to being cold for that matter. With no central heating in her parents' sprawling home, she'd learned to bundle up in the winter. But she thought winter had passed by. Now she felt hurled backwards as if she were snowballing down a hill.

She thought about the hot chocolate she had agreed to warm for the hotel's patrons. She must get busy.

Like the windmill back on the farm her mind spun to the kilts she'd admired—the tartan pleated kilts that the hotel's female employees wore. When the women walked, the skirts seemed to dance behind them. A lovely sight. Although Dat would find them flirtatious no doubt.

As her thoughts twirled and zigzagged, she considered the idea of a man wearing a kilt. Apparently at one time this was common. She'd seen men dressed thusly in paintings on the hotel's walls. Would Alec do such a thing? She chortled as she imagined his hairy legs hidden under long stockings. Hush, she said to herself. Her dat would consider this sinful thinking.

Ach, she'd forgotten to bring a cup of hot chocolate to the room for herself. As she descended the stairs and headed back to the kitchen, she heard voices and laughter. She made her way toward the conversation using a flashlight Molly had lent her to illuminate her path.

Then all went silent. Using what her mam called "quiet feet," she tiptoed into the kitchen. Ahead she saw a couple holding hands making their way inside.

"I'm sorry," flew out of her mouth before she could stop herself. She had nothing to be sorry for. Regret was her initial reaction to everything.

It appeared that Alec was leading Denny by the hand. Both gawked at her. Their faces wore a look of surprise, as well they should. Lydia was shocked. Hadn't those two just met each other only hours earlier? They were practically strangers. Not that Lydia wouldn't want to be in Denny's place. Ever since first seeing Alec, she had been attracted to him.

"Something we can do for you?" Denny asked, not releasing his hand.

Lydia despised Denny's haughty tone of voice. At this moment, Lydia disliked everything about Denny. But she would be forced to share a room with this horrible woman. What choice did Lydia have? Her mind whirled with ways to escape this awkward situation, but she came up empty.

She gathered her courage and glanced over at Alec, who was backstepping away from Denny. Lydia wondered if Denny had grabbed hold of his hand the way his other arm hung at his side so limply. Clearly, he was uncomfortable or embarrassed.

Alec filled in the blanks. "She was having trouble walking on the icy path."

"That's too bad." Lydia wanted to laugh. Men were so gullible to a woman's guiles.

Mrs. Ross stepped into the room holding a flashlight. "This kitchen is as cold as an ice chest. What are you all doing in here?" She flashed her beam into Lydia's face. "Weren't you going to make hot chocolate? Oh, never mind, I see you did. Best go to bed."

"Yes, Mam—I mean madam," Lydia said. "I only wanted to help."

"I think we've had enough help around here for one night."

"You certainly can't blame the snowfall on my sister," Denny said. "Or the electricity outage. Or the fact that you have no fuel to run the generator. Alec and I just went out there to check it, and you have no gasoline, or whatever you run the machine with." Denny sounded as ornery as Dat's bull that had never been polled so its horns were hazardous. Which brought a smile to Lydia's mouth. Always her thoughts returned to her parents' farm. Both fond and bad memories.

"But she turned on the oven without first looking inside," Mrs. Ross said. "The smoke came out so quickly. And she calls herself a professional chef."

"Because she is." The corners of Denny's mouth tugged back into a grimace. Then she pressed her lips together into a flattened line. "How dare you demean her behind her back?" Denny said. "My sister paid good money to stay here in the dark and cold." Her hands clamped her narrow hips. "If any of us get sick, it will be on your head."

Lydia was glad Alec was seeing Denny for who she was. Bossy and belligerent under her sophisticated and creamy surface. The real Denny was exposing herself for all to see. Yet in many ways, Lydia admired Denny's audacity. Lydia would never have the courage to let her thoughts fly out of her mouth like wasps from a nest. Lydia was trapped inside a meek Amish woman's body. Just like her subservient mam, who would never speak back to Dat. Why, he was a minister of their district and commanded respect and obedience for the rest of his life. Her poor mam.

And what would be Lydia's fate? To always serve others. She recalled one Sunday last year listening to a minister speaking about Jesus washing the disciples' feet. Simon Peter had argued that he shouldn't, but Jesus insisted on serving Peter even as death's jaws approached. Lydia knew her rebellious nature was not what God wanted for her, but she enjoyed stretching her wings as it were and letting others serve her. Not that when it came to looking after Amanda and tidying up the Cooks' palatial home, she wasn't a hard worker. Ach, was she fooling herself? The truth was she had become lazy and was happiest watching TV and playing video games with Amanda—after helping the girl with her homework. Amanda's homework from a college prep school was a cinch for Lydia. That's why she figured she could pass the GED test and maybe even earn a scholarship to college. Her teacher in the one room schoolhouse had told Lydia was that she was bright. Brighter than bright.

Or was she fooling herself?

"Lydia?" Denny said. Lydia realized she was staring into nothingness.

Lydia spun around and walked right into an open wire cabinet housing dishes, teacups, and plates that shattered to the floor. The crashing sound echoed throughout the room.

"Are you okay?" Alec asked.

"Yah." Lydia froze for fear of stepping on a shard or knocking over something else.

"Be careful," he said.

"I can't believe it." Mrs. Ross shone her flashlight across the floor. "Who's going to clean up this mess? And pay for the damages?"

"I'm so sorry." Lydia felt mortified. She was glad the room was dim; she could feel her cheeks flooding scarlet red. What would she tell Maureen when Mrs. Ross presented her with a bill? Maureen might fire her. Maureen might leave her here.

"Hold on," Alec said. "That was an accident. I saw the whole thing."

Denny did not come to her aid as Lydia hoped she would.

"A clumsy accident," Mrs. Ross snapped. "I could lose my job."

"I'm sure it won't come to that," Alec said.

"I will take the blame because it was my fault." Lydia felt her heart pounding against her chest like a caged bird. At home she would not be punished if she were repentant and cleaned up the shards. But she would pay her parents back for the loss. How could she possibly do that in this instance?

"The snow will let up, and all will be well in the morning." Lydia repeated something she had read in a book or seen in a movie. Fiction.

"If anything, the weather's getting worse." He shined his flashlight out the window. "The snow's increasing, and the temperature's dropping."

"What if the pipes break?" Denny asked.

Mrs. Ross let out a gasp. "Oh no, I hadn't thought of that."

"I'm no plumber, but I've heard it's good to let cold water drip during a freeze." Suddenly Denny was a professional?

"Good idea." Alec turned on the water to a slow drip.

"How many guests are left in the hotel?" Denny asked.

"Just you and your sister and her daughter and one couple on their honeymoon."

Mrs. Ross rubbed her chin. "The rest took off. Not that I blame them. I'm glad we were not booked to capacity."

Denny chuckled. "The newlyweds will keep each other warm."

"We'd better send someone up to make sure they have enough wood for their fireplace." Mrs. Ross sounded in a tizzy.

"I'll do it." Lydia was glad for an excuse to leave the room.

"I'll help you," Alec said.

"No." Denny's voice cut in with authority. "First Lydia should clean up her mess here in the kitchen so no one hurts themselves. I'll help Alec bring in wood. Many hands make light work, right?"

"That sounds like a better plan." Mrs. Ross handed a broom and dustpan to Lydia. "Get to work. Sweep up every piece." She tugged over a plastic garbage bin to Lydia's side.

"While I help Alec." Denny reminded Lydia of a she-cat in her dat's barn.

"Whatever you like," Alec said, not sounding enthusiastic to Lydia's way of thinking. Not sounding enthusiastic at all. Lydia couldn't help but wonder if he wouldn't choose her over Denny under different circumstances. Her imagination took flight, and she envisioned herself in his arms. But the reality was that he might not find her attractive.

Lydia had spent long periods of time staring into the mirror in Amanda's bathroom, pretending she was a princess in a storybook or a glamorous actress in one of Amanda's TV shows. A waste of time if ever there were one.

Chapter 25

Denny followed Alec and Mrs. Ross to the woodshed behind the hotel's back exit. Fatigue blanketed her, but she told herself that moving would warm her if nothing else. She was used to going to the gym to exercise. So surely carrying armloads of wood upstairs would be a great way to keep herself in shape and warm herself too.

"Go back inside," Alec told Mrs. Ross, and she was quick to obey.

The snow continued to float to the ground like cotton puffballs. Denny could kick herself for not bringing along additional warm clothes, but how would she know? She'd checked the weather forecast before leaving New Jersey, where the temperatures there had been on the chilly side but not below freezing. Why couldn't Maureen have chosen to take them to a tropical island? The Bahamas.

Wait a minute, Denny never would have met Alec. She could care less if he was from clan MacDonald. She watched him gather an armload of chopped wood with ease.

"Save some for me," she said, hearing a flutter in her voice. Yes, she was definitely flirting with him. But what harm in it? She had quit shivering.

He glanced back to her and said, "Are you sure you want to help? I can take care of it."

"Yes, I could use the exercise. This cold air is refreshing." Not really, but she would need to change her attitude in order to spend time with him. She would need to change her attitude about

84

many things. What was the use of starting up a relationship with a man if she could be on the verge of death? And would she really want to live here with him? It was doubtful that he would move to America to be with her.

Whoa there, she thought. She was getting way ahead of herself. He had shown no interest in her other than keeping her from falling on the slippery snow. He had asked her nothing about herself, but then that was typical for men as far as Denny could see. Even her own father had shown little interest in her bookstore. In fact, he'd mocked her numerous times for what he called throwing money down the toilet in such an idiotic endeavor as a used bookstore.

He'd guffawed. "Who in their right mind would buy a used book to begin with when they can buy it new online?"

"Lots of people enjoy reading used books." Denny knew that arguing with him was pointless.

"Then they can go to the public library." Not that he had a library card and ever went himself. He cleared his throat. "I don't have time for reading anything other than market reports and emails. I get up early and follow the market. It's a dog-eat-dog world on Wall Street."

"But on the weekends?" she asked.

"On a good day I golf with prospective clients."

Finally, she gave up verbally sparring with him. Because she was the dummy who liked secondhand books. And no use wasting her gray matter on him anymore because he was dead. A tragic reality that sent a jolt through her each time she allowed herself to dwell upon it.

Her mother had often come to Denny's defense when he was giving Denny a bad time—as if they were in a court room. But she was gone too. No one left to defend her.

Denny told herself to quit reworking that impossible puzzle in her brain. She had spoken to Maureen about their death to no avail. It seemed as if Denny were pounding nails in Maureen's ears when she mentioned their parents, so why bother? Maureen had a husband and a daughter and could not understand the loneliness that Denny endured.

"Coming, lass?" Alec's question seemed to wake Denny out of a dream.

"Yes, sorry."

He handed her part of his load—only a few chunks.

"Where to first?" Denny felt reckless, as though she would follow him anywhere.

"Your sister's room."

Denny envisioned Maureen cuddled up in bed with Amanda. And what about Lydia? She might be in there too. "Sure, let's warm up my sister's room first."

They found the right room, number 205. He rapped on the door with his knuckles.

"It's just Denny and Alec bringing you wood for the fire." He spoke through the door. "Unlock the door and let us in."

The door rattled, then opened. Amanda peeked out and shined her flashlight in Denny's eyes. "Hey, Aunt Denny."

Denny blinked and recoiled from the piercing light, but she gathered herself and smiled. "Howdy, Amanda and Maureen. Isn't this fun, like a sleep out?" Denny had never used the word *howdy* before. Surely there must be a Scottish way of greeting people. She would have to ask Alec later.

"I hate camping, and you know it." Amanda spun away and dove feet first into bed burrowing under the quilt. "Burr, I hate being cold."

"You poor thing." Maureen tucked Amanda in. Amanda snuggled next to her mother, which Denny imagined was a rare occurrence.

Denny knew Amanda was not an outdoorsy girl. Quite the opposite. She loved basking in the sun and always kept the heat turned up too high. Nothing Maureen and Denny hadn't done at that age. Denny knew she'd been a pill, but Mom had accepted her adolescent behavior as normal. She was never critical. If Mom was alive, Denny would thank her. But too late now.

Alec set several split logs into the hearth atop the glowing coals. "Maybe more wood in your fireplace will help warm things up in here."

"You're planning to heat the whole building this way?" Maureen sat in bed watching. She pulled her covers up around her neck. If Denny wasn't mistaken, Maureen still wore makeup. Was she expecting a member of the press to arrive and snap her photo again?

"One room at a time." Alec averted his eyes. "Where is Lydia?"

"I sent her back to her and Denny's room."

"We'd better go down there next," he said.

"She told us she was used to sleeping in the cold and liked it that way," Maureen said, much to Denny's relief.

Denny had a better idea. "In that case, why don't we go visit the newlyweds next."

When Denny and Alec found the right room, there was a Please Do Not Disturb sign on the door. They both stopped short and chatted about their options. Finally, Alec rapped on the door and said, "Hullo. We have wood for your hearth."

"Could you please leave it outside the door?" a man's muffled voice answered, followed by a woman's titter.

"Of course." Alec set his armload of wood on the hallway floor. Denny could make out a grin on his face.

The two of them trotted downstairs to collect more wood. Denny hesitated to return upstairs but realized she had no control over Alec and Lydia. If they were longing for each other, Denny would just have to live with it. Another disappointment, but what else was new?

Trundling back up the stairs carrying wood, Denny's feet felt as heavy as if she were wearing lead boots. Much to her surprise and embarrassment, she found herself tearing up. She figured her tears had little to do with Lydia. But she simply could not take another disappointment.

"Anything you wish to share?" he asked, startling her. "If I'm not being too nosy."

"No, nothing." She sniffed.

"I'm a good listener."

What did she have to lose? She was tired of keeping her grief bottled up.

When she didn't respond to him, he said, "Maybe you should be speaking to your sister. Would you feel more comfortable with that?"

"No, she has enough problems of her own. And we share one of them." Denny felt a sob erupting from deep inside. "Both of our parents were killed in a car accident not long ago. Hit-and-run." Denny was overcome with sadness as if a giant had whisked her off her feet. "Someone ran their car off the road. Whoever they were fled the scene like a thief in the night."

"You think it was deliberate?"

She shrugged and found her shoulders had turned to stone. "No witness got the license plate number. The other car—apparently stolen—slowed down for a moment and then sped up and took off."

"I am so sorry." He curved his arm around her shoulder, and she leaned into him.

Though it was dark, she watched his features grow closer. His lips parted and neared her mouth. She luxuriated in his approaching kiss.

In a flash, candlelight exposed them. "Hi, Lydia. What are you doing here?" Denny's voice came out like a dagger. The intimate moment was shattered. Gone. Alec released Denny, much to her distress, and he stepped away. She wiped under each eye and glared at Lydia. Not that Lydia could see her clearly.

"I came to get wood and to make sure you were alright," Lydia said.

"As you can see, I'm perfectly fine." Denny was anything but fine. She had just spilled her guts to a stranger. She should have gone to the grief counselor her doctor had recommended when Denny mentioned her insomnia. But Denny had decided those groups were for losers and sissies. Yet when she got back home, she might make an appointment. But what good would that do? Her parents were gone forever. And her bookshop was a failure. She might as well close shop and find a nine-to-five job the way her father had admonished her to. Denny lacked business savvy. If only Dad was alive to advise her.

"I'll bring you wood." Alec's words harpooned Denny back to the present. "You two go to your room."

"You don't need my help?" Denny felt dismissed.

"Actually, I can move faster by myself." Proof positive he wanted to rid himself of Denny.

"We'll be fine," Lydia said. "I'm used to building fires and living without electricity."

Denny held her tongue as snappy comebacks threatened to spew out.

"I'm planning to come down in the morning and prepare breakfast," Lydia said. "Something special for the newlyweds depending on what's in the kitchen."

"On a gas stove top and oven no less," Denny said.

"Yah, just like at home." Lydia's face took on a look of panic, her mouth opening. "What used to be home anyway."

Chapter 26

Maureen enjoyed the feel of her daughter's arms around her, even if Amanda was doing it only to keep warm. Maureen did not miss the blare of the TV or music playing. When they got home, she would put down her foot and curtail the amount of TV Amanda watched daily, even if her daughter did put up a stink.

The word *hypocrisy* came to mind because after all, didn't she make her living on TV? Until last week anyway. She envisioned her life as a stay-at-home mother but couldn't make sense of it. What would she do all day? How would she entertain herself?

Amanda stretched and then murmured something in her sleep. Maureen had no idea what Amanda might be dreaming about. In truth, Maureen knew little about her daughter's life. She wondered if Amanda confided in Lydia. Yes, Lydia probably knew more about Amanda than Maureen did. She had been a crummy mother when it came down to it.

Amanda murmured something else then snuggled into Maureen for warmth. She pulled up the quilt to cover her darling child's shoulder. Maureen shuddered to think she'd even considered aborting her precious girl after days of gut-wrenching nausea.

Her mind skipped back in time. She'd grown tired of her old steady boyfriend, Rusty. Such a sweet guy but he couldn't compare to James. On the first few dates with James, he made it clear he only wanted casual sex. A fling. She'd gone along with his agenda—after too much to drink—only to find herself pregnant.

Maureen still remembered their horrendous conversation when she admitted she was expecting a baby.

"You're not on the pill?" he'd asked, incredulous.

"No, you're my first." Her second, anyway.

"Yeah, right." He snorted a chuckle. "You're just trying to force me to marry you."

"Not true." Maureen couldn't look him in the eye. "Never mind I'll raise the child on my own." She'd hoped her parents would help her. And she'd get a job. Maureen wanted it all. A career that took off like a rocket at Cape Canaveral. And a child. And if honest with herself a husband. She was confident she'd found a man like her father. Honest and dependable. She was saturated with optimism when she looked at herself in the mirror and considered her many talents.

"I'll eventually get married," she'd told James. "Another man will raise your child, call him Daddy."

"Now wait a minute." James stroked his jaw. "Not so fast. Are you sure I'm the father?"

"Yes, absolutely sure."

"Then you'd better get cracking. Find a church and a place to celebrate."

"Seriously?" She couldn't believe her good fortune.

"Yes." He'd held her close and whispered into the top of her head. "I'm falling in love with you."

She'd called her mother to tell her the good news. "Mom, I'm getting married." She paused. "I need to do it right away, if you catch my drift."

"Wonderful, darling." Her mother sprang into action as if she'd been waiting for this moment.

Maureen smiled as she recalled her bodacious actions and decisions. She had not minded losing her trim figure and blowing up like a balloon as long as James would marry her.

The flames hissed and crackled in the hearth. Maureen's inner clock was turned on its head. It wasn't the first time she'd suffered from jet lag. She and James had traveled throughout

Europe often. When Amanda was young, Maureen had hired a nanny. But she was glad she had not left her daughter home with Lydia this time. She needed Amanda too much. Which she knew was wrong. A daughter should need her mother not the other way around. Maureen needed her own mother very much. It hurt to think like an orphan. She wondered if Amanda loved her that much. Most of the time, her daughter seemed oblivious. Maureen knew it was her own fault. She had been so obsessed with her fantastic career. A career that was plummeting to an end.

She recalled a bird flying into the glass window at home. It sat there stunned, unable to move. But when Maureen had looked later, the bird was gone. She liked to think that it had flown away, but for all she knew, a neighbor's cat or a crow had killed it.

Amanda struggled with the covers. "Are you looking at me?" she asked.

Maureen knew her daughter was always in a bad mood when she first woke up—like a grizzly bear coming out of hibernation. But the flames casting a warm light across the bed gave Maureen courage.

"Can't sleep, darling?" Maureen asked.

"Not when you're staring at me."

"I was just thinking about how beautiful you are. And how much I love you."

"I'm ugly, and you know it." Amanda rolled away from her.

"That's not true."

"And fat."

Maureen, the plumpest member of the family, stiffened. "If anything, you're underweight. How on earth can you think you're fat?"

"Well, for one thing, I'm pregnant. Can't you tell the difference?"

"But you don't even have a boyfriend."

"Shows how much you know."

"But how could this happen?"

"Duh. Like how dumb are you? Do I need to teach you the facts of life?"

"But I hired Lydia to look after you."

"She goes to the grocery store. Sometimes she's gone for hours. And you and Dad are never home."

Maureen had never been more taken aback. She reminded herself that she hadn't told her own mother the truth. She would do anything to have Mom's sage advice right now.

Chapter 27

When Maureen stormed into the room and yelled, "Lydia, you're fired," Lydia cowered. What had she done? Did Amanda's father call to inform Maureen about the dent in her car when Lydia was driving it? Had law enforcement tracked down her whereabouts and demanded her return to the States immediately?

"What gives?" Denny asked. "Missing the scarf and earrings that Lydia swiped from you?"

"No, I gave those to her as gifts."

"Lydia's calamity in the kitchen?" Denny asked.

"No, this is something far worse." Maureen's cheeks turned an angry fiery red.

Denny folded her arms. "You want to let me in on this?"

"I hired Lydia to look after Amanda, not look the other way."

"What could be so bad?" Denny asked in her usual blithe manner. "Something to do with your TV show?"

"No, that's relatively insignificant. Small potatoes." Maureen hunched over. "Oh, Denny, I've been such a terrible mother."

"What are you talking about?" Denny's brow creased. "You're a wonderful mother. And what does this have to do with Lydia?" She wagged her head. "Don't tell me she and Jimbo have something going on."

"Not that I know of. But from what Amanda said, I can't rule out anything."

The words *You're fired* reverberated in Lydia's ears. Maybe

94

this was the Lord's way of keeping her here. But also of never seeing her family again.

Lydia slipped out of the room before Maureen could speak of her again. In the dark hallway, Lydia walked right into Alec. Molly hurried by following Alec's flashlight beam.

Lydia heard the words *Princess* and *puppies*. Wanting to be as far away from Maureen as possible at the moment, she followed Molly and Alec, hastening to keep up.

How exciting was all she could think. Lydia was a lot more capable at helping birth animals than she was raising Amanda, who wasn't anything like the children in her family or church district. Eventually, Lydia would have to face Maureen and her accusations but not now when she might be needed by Princess. If Princess even needed her help. On the farm, animals often gave birth at night without anyone's assistance. Barn cats seemed to be quite capable, but as she recalled someone always helped their dogs whelp their puppies. She thought of her dat's many barnyard skills that he never spoke about. She could remember his reaching inside a cow to turn the calf around the right direction before the veterinarian could arrive.

Yet sometimes the process went wrong, and the animal was born lifeless. She wished her dat were here right now not on the other side of the ocean.

Crazy thinking is what she was doing. Her mind was spinning in circles, but she kept up with the two ahead of her. Even in the shadows, she could make out Alec's confident stride.

They stopped short when they reached the kitchen. Lydia almost ran into them.

"Please, Molly," Lydia said, "fetch some towels, and warm some water on the stove."

Ahead, Lydia could make out the silhouette of Princess as she paced and panted. Standing in the whelping box, she dug into the newspaper, then turned in a circle and lay on her side.

Molly returned carrying towels. "Do you think she's okay?" she asked.

"No idea." Alec's voice was low and sober. "But I doubt we can get a veterinary doctor here in time to be of any use."

"How long has she been like this?" Lydia asked.

"A couple of hours?" Molly said. "I wasn't paying attention."

Lydia stroked the dog's underbelly and guessed Princess would give birth to three or four puppies. If they all lived.

She prayed silently: please, Lord, help Princess. Lydia's hand felt another contraction, and she hoped the Almighty really did love all creatures great and small. This last year Lydia had been so disobedient. Why would God answer her prayers?

Another contraction and Princess let out a sound that reminded Lydia of a bawling calf.

"The first one's coming," Lydia said, attempting to keep her voice soft and soothing. The last thing she wanted to do was agitate Princess.

Indeed, a puppy emerged. Princess licked the pup still encased in its placenta and broke it open. Princess licked the pup's mouth and nostrils so it could breathe.

"It's breathing." Lydia felt like weeping with joy. She knew from watching the animals back at the farm that this was a moment of life and death for both mother and baby. Lydia took hold of a towel and dried off the puppy briskly.

She wished Amanda could watch this miracle of life but didn't want to disturb Princess, who had started panting again. All three people in the room fell silent as another contraction took hold of Princess like an ocean wave. Princess moaned as another pup emerged. Mama dog repeated the process.

In an hour, Princess had birthed three perfect puppies.

"You were incredible, Lydia," Alec said.

"Not me," Lydia said. "Princess did all the work."

He chuckled. "I'm guessing that's why they call it *labor*."

The three puppies suckled from their mother who continued to lick them. Then Princess flopped her head to the side and rested.

"I hope this room is warm enough." Lydia felt Alec's presence close behind her. She wondered if Alec might kiss her. She would be thrilled if he did, but he seemed intent on the puppies—not on her.

"I'll stoke the fire," he said.

"Good idea," Denny said.

"Denny?" He swung around. "How long have you been standing there?" Alec asked.

"Ten minutes, but I didn't want to bother Princess. And it seemed as if Lydia had everything under control." Denny hovered in the darkness. "Well done, Lydia."

"*Danke.*" Lydia knew she had done very little. Her dat would say that pride is a sin. But she was proud of herself. She sighed because she couldn't win.

In a jolting flash, the lights came back on, illuminating the room and making everyone squint. Lydia could hear the furnace kick on.

"Good," Denny said. "It should be eighty degrees in here."

"How do you know so much?" Lydia asked.

"From a book I read at my bookshop." Denny stepped closer and rested a hand on Lydia's shoulder in a way that seemed so loving it startled Lydia. "Looks like you have personal experience in these matters," Denny said.

Lydia looked up at her. "Yah, I do, but she would have done fine without me."

"Maybe."

Lydia was glad to see that Denny didn't reach out to stroke Princess, who might bite her under the circumstances.

"My best guess is that she needs water and food," Denny said and turned to Molly. "Do you know where they keep her kibble and dishes?"

"Yes, I'll be right back." Molly slipped out of the room.

Lydia was surprised to find a tear in her eye. She had no idea why. Because Alec had failed to kiss her? Because Denny had once again taken over? Lydia felt a battleground of conflicting emotions warring in her heart. She missed her parents, even if they were disappointed in her. She longed to be back in familiar surroundings.

"When I return to America, I'm taking one of the puppies with me." Denny spoke as if it were a done deal.

"What if the owner isn't willing to sell you a pup?" Alec asked and received a shrug and return. "Knowing Gordon, I doubt he will. Especially if he discovers you're a Campbell."

"I'll find a way to convince him." Denny pointed to the lighter-colored pup in the middle. "I want that little girl. And I'll name her Rosie."

Lydia wondered how Denny knew it was a female from so far away.

Alec saved Lydia from having to ask. "How do you know that's a girl?" he asked Denny, who leaned over and examined the puppy. Princess didn't seem to mind the intrusion, but she did lick the pup thoroughly after Denny was finished checking it.

"Just as I thought, a little girl." Denny's grin expanded. "When you're hot."

Lydia felt like throttling her. But Amish were pacifists, Lydia reminded herself. "Turn the other cheek," the minister had told everyone during a sermon at church last year.

What had gotten into her?

Chapter 28

Denny was super excited about her new puppy. She could barely contain her happiness. The name Rosie had crystallized the moment she saw the precious pup. Her new soulmate. She'd do anything to bring the pup home with her, even if it meant returning in two months. How Denny would pay for Rosie she had no idea.

Denny's arm brushed against Alec's, and she felt a tingling spark of vitality. Oh yes, she had the hots for him. She wished she'd taken advantage of the darkness when she had his full attention. If nothing else, they could have shared a hug or a brief kiss.

She reminded herself that he'd given little indication how he felt about her. She'd heard of long-distance dating. But traveling across the Atlantic Ocean to go see a show together would be an impossible arrangement. She could move to Skye. But no way could she stay here with her little bookshop unattended. Unless she sold it. Was it possible there was a buyer out there looking for a used bookstore? Unlikely. She was getting way ahead of herself, as always. She hardly knew Alec. And she sensed there was a connection between him and Molly. A bond that would not be broken by Denny or any other tourist.

What an idiot she was to think she could move here to be with a man she hardly knew. She would go home to her drab life and continue plodding along as usual. Same old, same old. Well, it was time to make a change to her routine. Should she buy a blond wig, learn to play the bagpipe, join the Amish church when they got home and live without electricity all year round every year? No that would be too drastic a change. She needed to take baby steps one at a time. Maybe sign up for that watercolor class a customer in the store had been speaking of.

Then she remembered her darling Rosie. Once back in the States, she'd be too busy taking care of her new pup. She'd be swamped between working at her bookshop and tending to Rosie's needs. When her pooch was old enough and had been thoroughly vaccinated, she'd take her to puppy socializing classes and then obedience school.

"Let's give this new family privacy," Molly said. She ascended the stairs. Lydia, and Alec fell in behind her.

Before Denny reluctantly followed, she took one last peek over her shoulder to make sure that the miracle she'd witnessed was real and not an illusion. Sure enough, Princess inspected and licked her pups.

Watching Alec climb the stairs, Denny's heart felt so full of joy it might burst. Everything she'd long for was here on the Isle of Skye.

When they reached the kitchen, Alec turned to Denny and said, "I hope you're not setting yourself up for a bitter disappointment. The hotel's owner and I get along just fine, but I must warn you, he's what I would call inflexible. Once he's made his mind up, there's no changing it."

Denny would not be deterred. "I'll find a way to convince him."

Chapter 29

When the power came back on, Maureen jerked. Her eyes squinted against the harsh light of the bulb in her bedside lamp. She hated losing her intimate time with Amanda, who sprang to life with glee.

"Yay, I can charge my phone now," Amanda said.

"Not so fast, we have to get the right kind of plug."

"Why didn't you bring one along?"

"I didn't think to, darling. Sorry."

Amanda snatched the hotel's bedside phone from its cradle. "Hello, I need a new plug to charge my iPhone."

"Someone will bring an adapter up—within an hour."

"A whole hour?" Amanda paused for a moment then slammed down the phone. She turned to Maureen. "They asked me not to use my plug, so I don't fry their electrical system. Which is a laugh since we've been without electricity." Amanda expelled a chuckle.

Minutes later Maureen heard a rap-rap-rap on the door. "Who is it?" Maureen asked, hoping to instill caution in her daughter, who would open the door to any stranger.

"Expecting someone special?" Denny asked.

"It's Aunt Denny," Amanda said with exuberance. She vaulted out of bed and was opening the door before Maureen could say another word.

Denny enfolded Amanda in her arms and kissed the top of her head. An act Amanda would never allow Maureen to do.

"What brings you by?" Maureen could hear a snarly twang

in her voice. She resented the fact that Amanda loved Denny so much. Maureen knew she was being childish. But Aunt Denny didn't have to deal with late homework assignments or any of the few household chores that Amanda was responsible for. What was Maureen talking about? Now that Lydia lived with them Amanda didn't have any household chores. And for all she knew, Lydia did Amanda's homework for her.

"Good news," Amanda said to Denny with buoyancy. "The furnace is back on."

"That is good news." Denny sent Maureen a wink. "And yet it's still snowing."

"It is?" Amanda flounced over to the window. "Mommy, can I go out now and play in it?"

Maureen cast Denny an imploring look.

Denny nodded. "Too late now, sweetie pie. First thing tomorrow we can go out and build a snowman and make snow angels."

"Promise?"

"Well, maybe not the first thing but soon after a cup of coffee and after I show you my big surprise."

Amanda looked up to Denny with wide eyes. "What surprise?"

"I'm getting a new puppy."

"What?" Maureen said. "Since when?"

"It's only a couple hours old so since it was born."

"I wanna see it right now." Amanda said.

"Not yet. Rosie's mommy wouldn't like it. She's terribly protective, as you can imagine she would be. But she'll get over that soon enough."

"Where did Princess have this puppy?" Maureen asked.

"She actually had three pups." Denny chortled. "Down in the basement, next to the room where Alec has been sleeping."

Maureen could not contain her laughter. "Oh dear, now I've heard everything."

"I guess she's been nesting in that area for several days, but

102

he didn't have the heart to boot her out, so he made a whelping box."

"How is it that you get to have one of the puppies?" Maureen asked.

"I just am."

"How, if it was born only hours ago?"

."I'll figure it out."

"But how?"

"Trying to rain on my parade?" Denny wagged her pointer finger at her sister. "You always do this when something good happens to me, and I'm supposed to go along and smile when spectacular things happen to you."

"Since when?" Maureen was baffled, but she didn't want to talk about her possible job loss in front of Amanda. Maureen would try to be happy for her little sister. That's what their mother would have done.

Even when their father berated Mom in public, she would form a placid smile on her face as if she hadn't a care in the world. As if he had said she was the most cherished and intelligent person in his life. Their mother had looked like a svelte movie star to Maureen. She'd taught Maureen everything she knew about cooking. But Denny had inherited their mother's genes when it came to good looks, including her slim figure. Sorting through their mother's clothes closet after her death, only Denny could fit into any of them with a little hemming.

Maureen's thoughts turned to James, who was arrogant when it came down to it and acted much like her father had. Which she'd always thought was a good trait. But she doubted if James cared a whit if she lost her job. He'd probably laugh with his buddies at the golf and country club. Anything to prove that he was superior to Maureen.

Maureen guessed he was, so no need to compete.

It occurred to her again that he had not tried to call her once. Wasn't he at least curious about her and their daughter? He kept a photograph of them on his mahogany desk at work. She wondered what his motives were for having it. Probably to make his clients feel at ease. She recalled the photo shoot. Everything had to be perfect. He'd even hired professionals to coif Maureen's hair and apply makeup to make her look better than she really was. She wondered if he mentioned to his clients that she was in essence a television star. Everyone loved food and cooking programs and eating gourmet food. Everyone loved Maureen's show, until a few days ago. Was that part of her life over? She recalled the kitchen of this hotel filled with smoke, proof that she was inadequate. She would have to reinvent herself. Maybe when they got home, she'd hire a career counselor. Or maybe be a stay-at-home mom. Be there when Amanda came home from school.

"Mommy, Mommy, are you listening?" Amanda shook Maureen's upper arm, bringing her out of her musings. "Did you hear one word I said?" Amanda asked.

"I'm sorry, darling. I must have dozed off."

"Well, can I? Aunt Denny says I have to get your okay."

"All right as long as you stick close to Aunt Denny." Maureen had no idea what her daughter wanted but didn't wish to admit that she wasn't listening. That her behavior was just as bad as James's.

"But not too early, okay?" Denny yawned. "The snow won't melt if we snooze in bed for an hour or two longer. And Lydia promised to prepare something special for breakfast tomorrow."

"I have her breakfast every day." Amanda folded her arms across her chest. "I will eat breakfast only if I can see the puppies first."

"We will have to wait and see how Princess is doing," Denny said. "She might still be protective of her pups."

"How did you decide on the name Rosie?" Maureen asked. She bet it had something to do with Alec. She'd sensed a buzz of attraction between the two. Denny had always been boy crazy. Almost without fail, Denny had gotten a crush on Maureen's boyfriends in high school and in then college. James was the one exception. Denny made it clear from the start she didn't care for him and vice versa.

"I want a puppy too," Amanda said. "Mommy, promise me when we get home we can get one. Please, please, please."

"You know your father is allergic to dogs. Even more so to cats."

Denny chuckled. "Likely story. Has he gone to an allergist?"

"He says they bother his asthma, and I believe him." Maureen hated Denny demeaning James in front of Amanda.

"Humph," Denny said. "He always looks healthy to me."

"Please, Mommy." Amanda's voice grew in intensity. "I want a cairn terrier puppy the color of Rosie. I wonder what we should name her." Amanda danced around the room, then flopped down on the bed. "I love the name Rosie."

"Is she pink?" Maureen asked Denny, feeling snarly.

"Ha-ha, very funny." The corners of her mouth drawn back, Denny did not appear to be amused. "She is a lovely light reddish-brown color and the sweetest of the sweet. I love the smell of puppies better than anything."

"Better than books?" Maureen asked. "Or newborn babies?"

"Hey, why are you always trying to hurt me?" Denny moved toward the door, took the handle. "Sometimes I hate you."

"The feeling's mutual, dear sister."

Chapter 30

Denny knew she had brought Maureen's wrath upon her. She considered turning around to apologize to her sister but was afraid she would retaliate. Most of her life she'd held in her anger. Maureen was trying to hurt her by reminding her she would always be an aunt and never a mother. Well, Denny would mother her new puppy. She already loved Rosie. The warmth in her chest expanded. This must be what motherhood felt like. Sure, she loved Amanda but imagined that having a child of her own would grow to greater intensity. Or not. Some children brought sadness and stress upon their parents. She imagined parents whose children had disgraced them and wondered if the parents still loved them. She would, no matter what they did or how they acted.

Finding her way back to the room was easy with all the hall lights on. But she preferred the darkness and recalled walking right into Alec's wide chest. Instead of stopping at her bedroom, she padded down the wide staircase and found the kitchen lights bright.

She located Lydia in the kitchen inspecting behind the stove.

"One last look?" Denny asked her.

"Yah, I'm searching for chards that might have found their way back here. Mrs. Ross expects the job to be done by now." She got to her feet and stood admiring the clean floor. "And I'm used to it. I hate to admit it, but I enjoy cleaning."

"You have got to be kidding." Scrubbing the floor would be Denny's least favorite pastime, but let's face it, a puppy would leave liquid and poopy messes for Denny to clean up. She

106

couldn't leave Rosie at home all day while she was at the bookstore. She envisioned her bookshop and decided she would put in a small pen near the register where Denny could keep a good eye on Rosie and bond with her. Rosie was sure to whine and bark, but her customers would just have to get used to it. She couldn't afford to hire a dogwalker or someone like Lydia the way her older sister did. And Denny didn't want to.

Recalling Maureen's cruel statements brought a crushing feeling to Denny's chest. Or had Denny started the spat? She couldn't remember. In any case their argument had spiraled down to the truth because in many ways, they had hated each other since childhood. Had Maureen ever loved her? Or had she resented Denny since her birth, while Denny had yearned for Maureen's approval as well as her parents' attention all her life? How pathetic to be such a people pleaser.

Alec strolled into the kitchen. "You two had better turn in," he said. "It's almost midnight."

Graceful Lydia stood with ease and turned to face him. But Denny moved between them. No way would she let this young woman steal Alec away from her. Not that she had him. And her future was shaky at best. Why hadn't she insisted her gynecologist see her again before she left the States? Knowing she would soon have Rosie to care for invigorated her. She needed to get healthy. But Alec was right. She needed to get some sleep, or she'd be a wreck tomorrow.

When Lydia left the room, Denny spoke to Alec who watched her exit. "I want to go down and peek in on the puppies before I turn in," Denny said.

"Aye, I'll take you. But then you must go to bed."

Denny and Alec descended the stairs to the basement. Denny detected a new bounce in her step as she followed him, but she cautioned herself not to read too much into the excursion. Who wouldn't want to see a brand-new litter of pups?

Denny supposed Princess might growl, but mama dog remained at ease. Denny reached out and stroked her behind the ears. She was dying to pick up Rosie and examine her more closely but decided she'd wait and let the adorable new family rest.

"Do you think Princess needs anything?" she asked Alec.

"It doesn't look as if she's finished what she was offered yet. I'll see she gets fresh water before I turn in," Alec said. "She seems to be content."

"Where will you sleep tonight?" Denny said.

"Asking for an invitation?" He sent her a wry smile.

Denny's hand flapped up to cover her mouth. "No—no," she sputtered. Not that she would mind one. She had been lonely too long. But she was not into one-night rolls between the sheets.

Her many losses played in the back of her mind like a movie she couldn't turn off. She was flabbergasted when she felt a tear forming in the corner of her eye.

Alec must've noticed because he said, "I'm sorry if I said something inappropriate."

"No, you didn't, it's just that…" Her throat closed blocking off her words.

Alec waited patiently for her to continue her thought. Where to begin? "You already know our parents died recently."

"Aye. Again, I'm so sorry for your loss."

"Thank you. And Maureen had this crazy idea that coming on this trip would draw us closer together—we've had a difficult relationship our whole lives— but we're further apart than ever." She dug her hand into a pocket and found a Kleenex and stabbed her nose. "On top of that, my bookstore is going under. When I get home, I may have to close it."

"Can't you borrow the money?"

"No collateral. At one time, my parents might've helped me. Although my father was always against my starting the business and thought it was a frivolous waste of time. Still, he might've lent me the money."

"Forgive me if I'm being rude in asking if your parents left you anything."

"An inheritance? I wish." She dried her eyes. "No pot of gold at the end of the rainbow waiting for me." She dabbed her dripping nose. "Maureen and I had no idea our parents had taken out a second mortgage and were living on a pittance." She blinked. "Maureen is paying for this whole trip, and we're not getting along to put it mildly. But I'm glad I came because I met you and Rosie—that's what I named my pup."

"I hate to bring you down, but like I said before, the owner of this hotel also owns Princess. Gordan is a crusty, inflexible gent. I doubt he wants to let any of the puppies go unless at a hefty price."

Denny felt herself sinking further into the mire. "I can't take another disappointment." Her knees weakened. He slid his arm around her shoulder. She sank into him, let him support her. She couldn't make it on her own, but soon she would have to.

Chapter 31

Lydia woke with a start not knowing where she was. She expected to smell the aroma of her mam's breakfast or the farmland fragrances and sounds she had come to know over her lifetime. She struggled to reach consciousness.

The air had been cool when she'd fallen asleep, but the room was now warm and toasty, thanks to the furnace. Would she have been content to live on the farm if her parents had a furnace? No, that was not the deciding factor.

Her thoughts meandered to Jonathan, and she felt an unexpected tingle. Yet she had not contacted him for months and months. He had no idea where she was. Her rebellious nature had refused to ask his permission. And why should she? If she married him, he would be the head of the household, and she would need his approval on everything. Not fair, she told herself. But Jonathan was not like her domineering dat, who had ruled the family with an iron fist. She supposed that's why Dat was such a respected and trusted minister.

She heard Denny's breathing turn jagged, and she flopped on her back. Having a nightmare perhaps. Lydia had endured enough of those. She wondered what Denny was dreaming about. Probably Alec. It was obvious that Denny was smitten with him. She was a beautiful woman, although Lydia doubted Denny realized that fact. And to be fair, Denny's parents had both died recently. Lydia should show more sympathy. Denny had cried and cried at the funeral—unlike Maureen, who'd remained stoic. And Maureen had let slip that Denny's bookstore was floundering, headed for bankruptcy.

Lydia wondered what it would be like to own a little shop. She could sell fabric and quilts, even if she didn't make them herself. In fact, she could quilt when business was slow. If she married an Amish man, the shop would be considered his, even if she ran it and did all the work. But so what, as long as she didn't have to muck out stalls. That was one thing she liked about Jonathan. He was soon to inherit his parents' cornfields. His father was retiring next month and moving into the *dawdi haus*, attached to the main house with a breezeway between them. Lydia actually liked his easy-going parents, and she knew they liked her and expected her to be their daughter-in-law. But she had found ways to delay their marriage. Now that she could drive a car, the Englisch life tempted her to join it rather than the Amish church with its hard wooden benches. She was enjoying this plush bed and quilts. But what would she do now that Maureen had fired her? Find another job and live in a sparse apartment house? Maybe Denny would share a small cottage with her. *Nee*, not Denny. Or she would leave an ad at the grocery store.

She glanced at the clock with its illuminated face blaring at her. Five already. Not that it was really five at home, but no matter. She had promised to help make breakfast and would fulfill her obligation. She turned on her bedside lamp and was glad to see that Denny had not been disturbed. Lydia found clean clothes—skinny jeans and a long-sleeved T-shirt—and then slipped out of the room, careful to close the door quietly. As she strolled down the hall and descended the stairs, she was surprised to hear voices ahead. Molly, a mug of coffee in her hand, greeted Lydia with a smile.

"Good morning," Lydia said. "How did you get here?"

"On foot. I live nearby with my parents. The snow has not let up. It's still coming down fiercely. But I thought I might be needed here."

"To cook?"

"No, I prefer to serve what someone else has prepared," Molly said. "I eat mostly raw fruits and vegetables. And fish."

111

She turned toward a white-aproned young man at the sink and dishwasher. "Malcolm here trudged through the snow to wash dishes."

A young man in his late teens with long, dark hair pulled back into a ponytail bobbed his head and grinned at Lydia, who raised a hand in return and sent him a smile. He reminded her of the neighbor's son back in Lancaster County.

"Have you come down to prepare the meals?" Molly asked Lydia.

"Yah, I thought I would help if the hotel was short on staff." Lydia wondered if she should run up and ask Maureen's permission, but Lydia doubted she would be awake yet. "I see someone has made coffee," she said.

"Malcolm did. Please help yourself." Molly poured some into a mug and handed it to Lydia.

"Any other new guests or employees show up while I was sleeping?" Lydia asked.

"No, like I said, the snow has increased, and a wind from the northeast has picked up. The worst storm I can ever remember."

"We have got to at least feed the newlyweds," Lydia said.

"They put a Please Do Not Disturb sign out and a card saying they wanted breakfast at nine. If it's available."

"Did they say what they wanted?"

"Yes, it's right here." Molly placed their order on the counter.

Lydia figured she could make anything on the menu. But Maureen might march down and take over. "Did anyone else spend the night in the hotel?"

"No. And I doubt our chef will come in until the roads are cleared. The way the snow is coming down that could be a while."

Lydia sprang into action. "I bet I can make everything on the menu plus a delicious breakfast casserole." She peaked into the stove before turning it on, then set a couple of skillets atop the stove. "What do you have on hand?" She opened the massive refrigerator door and found cheese, ham, and onions. Moments later she was chopping onions and preparing her casserole. Her eyes teared up. She imagined herself as Jonathan's wife and fixing him breakfast. He would have already gone out and milked their one cow in the barn and brought in fresh eggs. Nothing could compare to the freshness of eggs and milk on a farm. But did she want to get baptized and marry an Amishman? Could she submit to the many Amish rules? Or was her new home here in Scotland?

"Oh no, I haven't put on the potatoes to boil." What had Lydia been thinking? Not enough time to cook and shred potatoes and then cool them.

"We have shredded potatoes in the freezer," Molly said. "Will they work?"

"I guess so." Although it felt like cheating. "I mean, yes please, that would be very helpful."

As Molly dug a bag of shredded potatoes out of the freezer, Lydia glanced out the window and saw the snow still falling and swirling in circles as gusts of wind kicked them up. At home it would be melting by now. "Does it always snow this much?" she asked Molly.

"My goodness, no. If anything, we get rain. And to my way of thinking, too much." Molly gazed out the window too. "But we do have freak snowstorms like this in early spring every decade or so. Let's hope this one is short-lived."

"Yah." Although Lydia could think of worse places to be stuck. She had never enjoyed such luxury.

Tousled-haired Alec stepped into the room. No doubt about it, Lydia found him attractive. Maybe *gorgeous* was a better word. But he seemed to look right through her as he made his way to the coffee urn. He served himself a cup, then splashed in half-and-half from a small carton.

"How are Princess and her puppies doing?" she asked him in an attempt to initiate a conversation.

"Fine." He gulped a mouthful of his coffee.

"She won't want to leave her puppies to go out on a day like today," Molly said.

"I'm afraid she has no choice."

Denny straggled into the room. "That java smells so good."

Alec poured her a cup, and she sent him a pretty smile. "What gets you up so early?"

"Lydia woke me." Just out of bed, Denny looked lovely.

Lydia cringed. "I'm so sorry. I tried to be quiet."

"That's okay, I couldn't sleep anyway."

"Want to come downstairs and stay with the puppies while I take Princess out?" Alec asked her.

"Absolutely." Denny rifled through the refrigerator until she found a carton of whole whipping cream to add to her coffee. She took a sip. "Lead the way," she said to him. "I can't wait."

Lydia listened to their words fade away. She would have loved to go downstairs with them but had not been invited. And she had a task to do right here. She had committed herself to making breakfast. She chastised herself for being so wishy-washy and lazy. She sighed as she located a clean white apron. Maybe her Amish heritage would stay with her forever. Maybe no matter where she lived, she would hear her parents' words in her ears.

As she sautéed the frozen potatoes in cooking oil, she broke the remaining clumps apart with a fork. Then she got to work shredding cheddar cheese. Minutes later she brought out eggs to beat. The faster she worked, the more she felt anxiety encompass her. She was used to using one hand to break an egg but found that she was not as skilled as she thought she was. Several cracked the wrong way; bits of shell fell into the bowl and sank below the surface.

If she were in her parents' home, she would turn to her mam and ask her what to do. Mam had a trick to extracting wayward eggshells. Lydia wished she could call her mother, but of course Mam did not have a cell phone nor was there a phone in the home.

Lydia's nerves were agitated. She forgot what came next in the recipe. She envisioned her mother's handwriting on a piece of paper, but she could not recall the ingredients or their amounts.

Living without phones or internet access in the home were many of the exasperating laws by which the Amish must live, Lydia thought. Her dat had explained this precept to her many times. The mandates were set in place to keep families and the community together. He would be so disappointed if he could see her now, floundering to make a dish that she thought she knew by heart. Ach, she would do her best because people were counting on her.

Molly watched her as she stirred her egg concoction. "You need this?" Molly brought out a rectangle baking dish. "Want me to grease it?"

"Yes, thank you so much." Feeling her heart lubb-dupp as if she had run up a hill, Lydia dumped the shredded potatoes into it and poured her egg concoction over them. Then she sprinkled the cheese over it.

"How long does it need to cook?" Molly asked.

"Only forty-five minutes. Then it needs to sit for ten more minutes."

"When it's done, I'll serve some to the newlyweds if they're up. I'll tell them it was made especially for them." Molly looked to the ceiling. "And we'll need porridge," Molly said. "The newlyweds requested it last night. A Scottish breakfast wouldn't be complete without it."

"I've never heard of that," Lydia said.

"It's what you call oatmeal."

Lydia canvassed the massive kitchen. "Would you please find the oats?" she asked.

"Sure. And we'll need ham cooked and bacon." She turned to leave. "Hold on. I'd better see what everyone has ordered first. What was I thinking?" She chuckled. "I normally work only at dinner time."

"A good idea." Lydia wondered how she'd manage the rest of the menu. She'd been proud of her cooking abilities, until now. She wondered if she could fulfill them. Her dat had taught her that pride—as opposed to satisfaction and happiness in a job well done—was a sin, and now she knew why. She had acted prideful.

She opened the oven's door and felt a burst of heat that made her eyes blink. She hoped she'd set the correct temperature. She would linger in the kitchen and keep checking on her casserole while Molly took orders, then brought the food to the dining room. But could the two of them manage? She hoped Malcolm could help.

Alec opened the back door and brought Princess back inside. The poor dog was caked with snow, but she tugged on her leash. When Alec unclipped the leash, she trotted down to the basement. Alec grabbed a clean towel and followed behind her. "I'm coming, lassie," he said.

He poured himself more coffee, then trotted down the stairs behind Princess. Lydia would have loved to follow him, but she had a job to do. A commitment she shouldn't have made. And yet she believed that helping others was pleasing to the Lord. In her mind, she saw herself doing such a fine job that the hotel would hire her full-time. Then she could move to Scotland. She had to wonder whether or not this was a zany idea. The way the snow was coming down and the wind blew, she figured she would have plenty of time to mull over the idea.

After ten minutes, Molly returned to the kitchen. "The owner called," she said, jerking Lydia into the present. "He said he can't make it in today, which is not so bad for us." She lowered her voice. "He's usually in a sour mood and brings with him nothing but negative vibes."

Lydia was shocked to hear Molly speak this way about her employer. Not that Lydia hadn't harbored negative thoughts about Maureen. Sure, Lydia was appreciative of Maureen for hiring her, but Lydia would never hire another person to raise her child. Maureen was devoted to her fame and TV program rather than her husband and Amanda. At least she'd brought Amanda on this trip with her. But her own husband would not come with her. What kind of a marriage was that?

Lydia's thoughts returned to her impossible dream of owning her own business, but she didn't have the start-up money to purchase inventory. If she were married, her husband could go to the bank and borrow it or might even give it to her if he was wealthy. These were issues that needed to be discussed before marriage. She did not want to die an *alde maedel*—an old maid. A spinster like her cranky but loveable great aunt.

As she gazed out the window at the continuous snowflakes backdropped by the lightening lavender sky, she thought of Maureen's stellar career, not that James didn't demean her as if she were a nobody. Lydia was glad he wasn't here. She avoided being alone with him the way he leered at her. He made inappropriate remarks to Lydia and told her off-color jokes. Or maybe she'd misunderstood him. Lydia was inexperienced with the ways of the world.

Not true, Lydia reminded herself. She had more experience than most. She was a thief who might go to jail for her criminal activities. She had been blackmailed for over a year, but that didn't make her any more innocent. She was not a child in the eyes of the law. If arrested for shoplifting and taken to court, the judge would show her no leniency. All the more reason to stay here on the Isle of Skye. She could not imagine that she would be extradited across the ocean for a pair of shoes.

She wished she could confide her many fears in someone she trusted. A lonely place to be, even if her hands were busy.

Chapter 32

Denny almost danced a jig she was so happy to see sweet little Rosie. Not that she knew how to dance Scottish style. But she just might learn the Scottish reel or jig while she was here. Who knew what her future held? Yet she warned herself that life and happiness were fleeting at best. Both her parents were dead, and she carried within her something lethal that her gynecologist and oncologist could not locate. How could her condition be treated until it was diagnosed?

She pushed the gloomy thoughts aside as she focused her eyes on Alec when he brought Princess back inside. Denny had better not rely too much on Alec either. She watched him as he towel-dried Princess. The warmth from the furnace melted the remaining snow from her fur.

Denny sat mesmerized watching Princess examine each of her pups and nestle in with them. Denny recalled how despite her childhood nagging her parents had refused to buy her a dog. Eventually, she'd attended college and studied English literature, much to her father's dismay. And he'd complained when she elected to open a bookstore. "You should work your way up the corporate ladder," he'd told her more than once. Every conversation turned into a lecture. The thought of laboring in the Big Apple and being a peon in a corporation held no allure to Denny. At heart she was a small-town girl. A single, small-town girl who liked to read. But she knew a man and a library full of books couldn't fix everything.

She reached down to stroke Rosie, and Princess gave Denny

the evil eye. "It's okay, mama dog," Denny said. "I won't hurt her. Not for anything." Then reality set in. She would have to wait at least eight weeks to transport her home. She'd have to find what the requirements were for importing a dog into the States.

"I wonder how much Princess's owner will charge me for Rosie," she contemplated out loud. Her savings account had been dwindling.

"If he'll sell her at all." Alec's serious tone revealed foreboding. He shifted his weight. "The hotel's owner's nickname is Old Man MacDonald. Some call him a grumpy old man and for good reason. Mr. MacDonald is rarely in a good humor. Maybe you could buy a puppy when you return to the States. There must be many kennels."

"That's probably a more practical idea, but I love this pup." She remembered Lydia's mentioning a cute but naughty cairn terrier everyone adored living in Lancaster County. "I'll speak to the owner when he makes it in." Denny was not ready to give up on Rosie. It's not as if they were going anywhere today what with this dump of snow. "Did the weatherman give any idea how long the snowstorm will last?"

"Apparently, it's not letting up for several days. Maybe longer. I feel badly about promising to drive you and your sister and her daughter around the island and then not being able to fulfill my obligation."

Denny was glad he hadn't mentioned Lydia, whom she expected would be his choice to spend time with.

Molly descended the staircase carrying a dish of dog food and fresh water, then turned on her heels and trotted back up the stairs. Princess's ears pricked, and her tail wagged. Denny admonished herself for not thinking of food and water first. She had much to learn about caring for a dog. She would have to get ready for Rosie.

"We'd better give Princess privacy," Alec said.

"I suppose you're right." Denny didn't want to leave.

"You're up early," he said.

119

"Insomnia. I've had it big-time ever since our parents' accident." In her mind, she finger-quoted the word *accident* because she'd wondered if the other vehicle had intentionally rammed into her parents' car. No, she'd watched too many thriller movies on TV and read to many mystery novels. Who would want to harm them? She envisioned the collision and shuddered.

She felt tears pressing at the back of her eyes but willed them away. No more pity parties.

"Another cup of coffee?" he asked.

"Good idea." She followed him up the stairs to see Lydia standing at the oven extracting a pan. "Something smells delicious," Denny said as they entered the kitchen. She wanted to show Alec that she had compassion for Lydia if she could. "Lydia, I'll help as soon as this coffee kicks in."

"That would be wonderful. I feel silly for forgetting the recipe." Chopped onions sat in a mound on the counter. "I can't remember what these onions are for."

"No matter, we'll think of something." Denny found an apron.

"I'll chip in and help you and Molly," Alec said, cinching an apron around his waist. "I worked in a restaurant in college. Together we can handle it."

Denny pursed her lips and held in her questions about why he had been expelled from college and had lost his scholarship. She guessed he lived with a mountain of disappointments and regrets too. Maybe everyone did.

Molly swished into the kitchen. She slipped her arm through his and glanced down at his apron. "What's this, are you going to help me serve breakfast?"

"If you trust me not to drop anything."

Denny thought the two of them seemed awfully chummy.

"How about if I serve the food and you pour them water, coffee, tea, or whatever beverage they'd like." Molly's lips wore a fresh coat of lipstick. "If they want hot chocolate, I can fix it in the kitchen. Or Lydia can."

"Yah," Lydia said. I will make them hot chocolate if anyone requests it."

"Sounds good," Molly said. "If you get buried in orders, one of us can come back and help you cook. Every time I take an order, I will put it right here." She pointed to a nail affixed to the wall. Once you make the item, please do remember to put the order slip in this basket so it doesn't get made twice. Make sense?"

"Yah, I understand and can do that."

"We shouldn't be busy today as there are few people left in the hotel," Molly said. "But you never know. My hunch is that schools are closed, so families may come out to eat. We'll have to wait and see."

The windows rattled as the wind kicked up. Denny glanced outside. Millions of snowflakes twirled to the ground. She'd heard each snowflake was unique. No two the same. She wasn't sure why this brought her solace. But it did.

Chapter 33

Maureen awoke with a start when Amanda squiggled out of bed and raced to the window. "It's still snowing," she said. She's sniffed the air. "Smell that? Bacon? Pancakes or waffles? No, I can't tell... toast?" She grinned. "Do you think they make Egg McMuffins like they have at McDonalds back home?"

"I don't know." Maureen had intentionally not put out a card for breakfast because she wanted to sleep in. She seemed to be tired all the time. Thankfully, Amanda had enjoyed a wonderful eight hours of sleep. But Maureen had tossed and turned as she worried about her daughter's pregnancy not to mention her husband's possible infidelity.

"I want some of whatever I smell." Amanda dove into clean clothes and headed for the door.

Maureen was ravenous too, but what else was new? "Wait, Amanda, honey, we need to talk."

"Later." Amanda sprinted out the door as Maureen splashed water on her face. No need for makeup in this hotel in the middle of a snowstorm. She was tempted to ask them to bring her meal to their room, but she needed to speak to Amanda. Maureen used the house phone to call Denny and Lydia's room but got no answer. She huffed as she thought of going to the trouble of getting dressed. She couldn't imagine that meddlesome reporter was anywhere nearby on such a bleak day. At one time, Maureen had welcomed the publicity but not today.

As Maureen strolled down the stairs to the dining room she berated herself for being such a crummy mother. Never at home.

Always busy. Thinking about herself and her career had dominated her life. She'd hired a nanny to raise her child. She deserved what she got. A cheating husband and a pregnant daughter.

Molly welcomed her. "Good morning. Would you like to sit next to your daughter?" Amanda had chosen a table by the window.

"Yes, thank you." How could Maureen be hungry knowing the crucial conversation ahead? But she was. She seemed to be a bottomless pit. Never sated.

"May I serve you tea?" Molly asked.

"No thanks. Coffee with a splash of half and half." She scanned the room an saw a dining room devoid of customers.

Maureen addressed Amanda. "Young lady, you and I need to talk."

"Before breakfast?"

"You dashed out the door so quickly or I would've spoken to you in our room."

"Always on my case for something." Amanda yawned without covering her mouth."

"How far along are you?"

Amanda stared back at her with vacant eyes. "What are you talking about?"

"Last night you told me you were pregnant."

"Oh that. I was just kidding."

"Teenage pregnancy is not a joke." Maureen wasn't ready to be a grandmother, yet she needed to know the truth no matter how gruesome. "Are you or are you not pregnant?"

"Not." Amanda seemed pleased with herself for fooling Maureen. "You bought into that? How dumb do you think I am?"

"Then why did you say it?"

Amanda smirked. "Just wanted to rattle your cage."

"But I believed you and fired Lydia because of it."

Maureen felt as though she'd been stung by a bumblebee. She was grateful her daughter wasn't going to have a baby in the near future, but she realized she'd fired Lydia without reason. She should've given the young woman time to defend herself.

Denny glided to the table wearing a white apron and carrying a carafe of coffee. She poured Maureen a cup. "I know what my sister likes."

"And how about me?" Amanda asked. "I want coffee too."

"You're too young." Maureen knew she was entering a losing battle.

"No, I'm not, Mommy. Please, half a cup? And don't tell me, it will stunt my growth. That's an old wives' tale."

Denny paused for a moment as if to get Maureen's permission. Then she poured half a cup of coffee for Amanda, followed by a slurp of milk. Maureen was not strong enough for another battle so early in the morning.

"How did you two sleep?" Denny seemed invigorated. She'd pulled her hair back into a sassy ponytail. Her voice was animated, she was wearing makeup and she looked cute.

Amanda's mouth puckered as she sipped her coffee "Aunt Denny, did you see that it's still snowing? I can't wait to go out in it. Want to have a snowball fight again?"

"A little later when I'm done helping here." Denny inspected Amanda's empty plate. "Hey, sweetie, what about breakfast?"

Amanda grimaced. "I'm not hungry anymore."

Maureen lowered her brows at Denny, who knew perfectly well that Maureen was devastated over the likelihood of her getting fired. Denny just grinned back at her as if she hadn't a care in the world. Maybe compared to Maureen she didn't. But had she forgotten about their parents' tragic deaths? Had she forgotten that her deadbeat boyfriend had dumped her and that she was still single and childless with her biological clock ticking down?

Maureen's dour mood did not stop her from eating until she felt like she was going to burst. Scrambled eggs, link sausages, baked beans, black pudding, scones, fried tomatoes and mushrooms, and toast. "I'll bypass the haggis."

"It's not on the breakfast menu," Denny said.

"Then I might try it some other time." Maureen could include the item in her new cookbook, which she envisioned as a possibility. She had to hand it to that reporter; he had a fantastic idea. Let the TV network drop her like week-old fish. She would have the last laugh. Over the years, Maureen had built up a large following. She had half-a-million followers on Instagram the last time she looked and assumed her book would be a great success when she got around to writing it. And if it didn't violate her contract with the network. She'd have a lawyer look over it when she got home. But not James, who would lord it over her if she lost her job. When she thought about it, he had never supported her. She was glad he wasn't on this trip, and she didn't miss him the tiniest bit.

Was Amanda right? Was her husband having an affair?

Denny strolled over to top off Maureen's coffee, but Maureen stopped her. "No more, thanks." Herbal tea sounded like a better option.

"How's your breakfast?" Denny asked her.

"Couldn't be better." Maureen dabbed the corners of her mouth. "I'm glad the cook made it to work."

"Our chef is Lydia." Denny smirked in a way that told Maureen she thought she had pulled a fast one.

"What?"

"She was nervous about taking the job on, but I encouraged her. And promised she wouldn't get in trouble. Will she?"

"No, not from me." Maureen spread marmalade on a piece of toast. "Denny, I feel so stupid. I fired her by mistake thanks to Amanda's prank. And I'll hire her back as soon as I can." She glanced up into Denny's grinning face. "How long have you been awake, little sister?"

"Several hours." Denny's smile widened. "Long enough to see my new puppy."

"Just how are you going to pay for this pup?" Maureen knew her words were barbed, but she was sick of Denny's pie-in-the-sky attitude."

"I was thinking you could lend me the money." Before Maureen could answer her, Denny spun away and returned to the kitchen, thank goodness. Maureen was in no mood for her flippant remarks.

"Why do you have to be so mean to Aunt Denny?" Amanda asked.

"I'm not mean."

"Yes, you are."

Maureen hunched over when she heard a thunderous roar followed by a thud. "What was that?"

"I want to go out and see." Amanda pushed back her chair and stood.

"It's still snowing. You need a jacket. And a hat."

"I'm not going to spend the day inside, mother dearest."

"But you haven't eaten breakfast."

"I'm not hungry. And I don't want to get fat."

Another loud thud shook the building.

"Be careful" was all Maureen could say as Amanda dashed out of the dining room.

Chapter 34

Lydia almost dove under a table when she heard the terrible thud and splintering of wood. If she had been at home, she would have thought the barn's roof had caved in due to the tremendous accumulation of snow. Something terrible had happened.

"*Vass in die velt*?" She lapsed into the Pennsylvania Dutch of her youth. "I mean 'What was that?'"

Molly shrugged. "Maybe snow sliding off the roof."

Alec loped into the room. "Everyone all right?"

"I think so," Molly said. "But on second thought that sound was more than snow falling to the ground."

"I heard it too," Lydia said. "I hope the roof hasn't caved in."

"The owner talked about making repairs last summer but never got around to it," Molly said.

"I'd better go upstairs and look around," Alec said.

"I'll come with you." Molly rattled a handful of keys. As the two left the kitchen, they were met by Denny, who insisted on accompanying them.

"Who will serve our patrons?" Molly asked.

"Lydia. But you'd better stay down here," Denny told Molly. "In case you're needed."

The corner of Molly's mouth curved up as she glanced to Alec. "I suppose you're right."

No food orders were waiting for Lydia's preparation, so she followed Denny and Alec up the stairs. Denny turned and scowled at her, but she ignored her. She had been content to work in the kitchen serving others for hours, but she was ready for a break and wanted to see what was happening, even if Denny didn't want her to. Except for a piece of toast with butter and honey, Lydia hadn't yet eaten breakfast. But she hadn't given up on Alec's attention. She'd noticed his gaze of admiration.

The three climbed another staircase and then another, this one steeper and narrower, meaning Denny practically rubbed against him like one of Dat's barn cats. But either he didn't notice or he liked it. Finally, Lydia saw they were in an attic, much like the one in her parents' home where her special trunk resided that Mam had been filling with linens, towels, and kitchen items since Lydia was a child for her future marriage. Her parents had assumed she would wed Jonathan, the only boy she'd ever dated or shown interest in. Although Lydia hated to disappoint her parents, she might have to do just that.

After they'd reached the attic, Alec looked to the slanted ceiling where water was dripping through a break in the roof.

"Now what?" Denny said.

"Now I call the owner and fill him in." Alec extracted a cell phone from his pocket and tapped in the number. "Hello, Gordon? It's Alec MacLeod here." He glanced up to the ceiling. "I hate to be the bearer of bad news, but I'm calling from up in your hotel's attic. You've got a nasty leak in the roof. My guess is from the weight of the snow." Alec paused. "I don't think the water's made it down to the guest rooms, but it's only a matter of time." Another pause. "Okay, we'll see you when you get here. Good luck."

"It sure is dusty up here," Denny said, then sneezed.

Lydia scanned the space illuminated by a single light bulb and saw tall back chairs and what must be upholstered chairs covered with sheets and old blankets. Stacks of cardboard boxes were labeled—water glasses, teapots, Christmas ornaments—that she would love to explore. She would return when the roof was patched and the leaking crisis was over.

Without a word, Lydia went to work emptying metal

containers filled with odds and ends—such as cloth napkins and silverware—and placed them under the spots that were dripping water, and then she moved items so they would not be damaged. Denny stood there watching. Surely Alec would see the difference between the two women, Lydia thought. She realized she was being prideful, but still her thoughts took on a life of their own.

"Pride cometh before a fall," her *grossmommi* often said. Lydia still heard her grandmother's wise words. Lydia's mam's mam was content—make that grateful—to live in the *dawdi haus* after her husband died in a tragic buggy accident ten years ago. The driver of the truck that hit his buggy had sworn that her grandfather wouldn't get out of the way when he honked at her *dawdi*'s buggy. The Englischer said that he had done his best to avoid hitting the horse and buggy when he passed it. Lydia recalled the funeral all too well.

"Oh, look, Christmas decorations." Denny's words harpooned her out of the past. No use moping over what Lydia could not change.

"With all this snow, this is like a second Christmas." Lydia thought of the Amish tradition. Not that her parents' home was ever decorated with sparkly ornaments. Lydia would have loved that bling, but her dat would have put a stop to anything more than sprigs of holly, evergreen, and mistletoe. Lydia smiled as she recalled Jonathan stealing a kiss under their mistletoe. Sometimes she really did miss him. Like right now.

She wondered what he was doing at this very moment. With the change in time, he might not be up yet to milk the one cow his family owned. Not much mucking to be done there, thankfully. Anyway, he had promised she would never have to muck out the barn. He really was a dear sweet man, and she guessed she loved him.

"What have we here?" Denny asked, extracting a blue cap wrapped in tissue paper from a box.

"Oh, please be extra careful with that," Alec said. "It's said to be once owned and worn by Bonnie Prince Charlie, also known as Prince Charles Edward Stuart, who sought to regain the thrown for his exiled father, James III, by invading Great Britain."

"Hmm," Denny said, "who was this guy?"

Lydia had read about him in school, but she kept her mouth shut for fear of Denny's barbed words.

"He's quite famous in these parts, even though he spent most of his life in Italy," Alec said.

"Why was he called Bonnie?" Denny asked.

"Also known as the Young Pretender, he is said to have had exceptionally good looks and charm. If he had been successful in his effort, then Great Britain would have most likely become Catholic again."

"It sounds like a tall tale or a romance novel."

"I wouldn't make light of him on the Isle of Skye," Alec said. "He's highly esteemed. There's a painting in the dining room of Bonnie Prince Charlie wearing this very hat." With care he took it from her. "Better wrap this up again. It belongs to the hotel's owner."

Denny sounded defensive as she glanced up at the dripping ceiling. "I might have rescued it from getting drenched. The owner might think I'm a hero."

"True enough." Alec rewrapped the cap in tissue paper and returned it to the box. "We'd better bring this downstairs and put it somewhere safe."

Lydia watched the back of Alec's head descend the stairs. His hair had a lovely wave to it and was the color of her dat's roan buggy horse.

"Ahem," Denny said as she scooted around Lydia and soon caught up with him.

Chapter 35

Denny wished she'd researched Bonnie Prince Charlie before the trip. But how would she know the importance he'd played here on the Isle of Skye? Or that she'd meet Alec. Meanwhile, Maureen was inhaling a book about Scotland's history. About Mary Queen of Scots. Well, no worries there because she already had a husband. Lydia was the one Denny fretted about snagging Alec's heart away. Molly might already own it.

She shook her head as she remembered that her life might be cut short prematurely. What was the use of starting a relationship with a man in Scotland? She felt helpless and frightened for her future. She should just call her doctor's office from Scotland. She could log into her medical account and find out what her test results were, but her doctor hadn't wanted her to. He'd insisted she enjoy this trip to the fullest. Which meant what? That he surmised it would be the last she'd ever take?

Like a cloud covering the sun, Denny's mood turned dark.

Amanda ran over to her. "Aunt Denny, come out with me. It's still snowing, but Mommy says I can't go outside alone."

"After another cup of coffee, sweetie." Denny turned to Lydia and said, "Isn't looking after Amanda your job?"

"Yah, of course it is." A smile bloomed on her blemish-free face. "Let me run upstairs and fetch my jacket and hat."

Denny noticed Alec's gaze turning to watch Lydia ascend the stairs two steps at a time. Danny was afraid that he'd follow her, but he didn't when he heard Mrs. Ross say, "Good morning to you."

"You spent the night here?" Alec asked her.

"Indeed, I did. I often take the bus home, but none came by, so I returned to the hotel and called Gordon. He insisted I stay and enjoy all the hotel's amenities." Her dimples accentuated her round cheeks. "How could I refuse?" She straightened her flyaway hair. "I think he had other ideas on his mind. That I'd continue to work, which is fine. I don't mind overtime."

"That's wonderful," Alec said. "I'm glad you're here because we're having a bit of an emergency. The weight of the snow was too much for the peaked roof. You've got a nasty leak above the attic."

"But I saved this." Denny gestured toward the box containing the cap, then wished she hadn't turned the spotlight on herself, like someone trying to outshine Alec and Lydia, who was trotting down the stairs wearing her coat and a red beanie. Denny assumed that acting like a show-off was not a quality Alec would find attractive. The opposite of humble Lydia.

"I mean, we all found it really," Denny said in an attempt to appear modest. "Alec is the hero for taking us up to the attic. I would never have thought to look up there when we heard that loud noise."

"I heard it too, luckily, or I'd still be sleeping." Mrs. Ross stifled a yawn with her hand.

"Come on, Lydia, hurry up." Amanda pulled Lydia's arm until she followed her out the front door. Lydia tugged down on her knit beanie. She looked beautiful even without makeup.

"Keep your distance from the hotel in case more snow slides off the roof," Alec said.

"Yes," Denny echoed. "Please be careful."

"You worry too much," Amanda said. "Worse than my mother." She ran out of the hotel's front door with Lydia close behind her. Both were chattering and laughing.

Moments later a sound like a locomotive filled the air. Denny glanced out the window in time to see white passing by. "Oh no. Was that snow?"

"Yes, from the roof." Alec raced out the front door with Denny on his heels. Both Amanda and Lydia had been knocked off their feet by the mini avalanche from the roof.

Lying on her back, Amanda's face, legs, and jacket were covered with snow. Her breath caught in her lungs as Denny scooped her up. "Are you all right, sweetie?" Denny hugged her. "Please tell me you're okay."

Amanda was visibly shaken but was breathing. "I-I think so."

Lydia lay halfway covered with snow. Alec ran over to her and pawed the snow off with his hands. Denny felt a sting of jealousy as he dusted the remaining snow off her face. Lydia was unresponsive.

"Wake up," Alec said. "Can you hear me? Wake up."

Lydia lay lifeless for a nanosecond, then finally stirred and murmured something Denny couldn't understand. Maybe in Pennsylvania Dutch.

"Thank the Lord," Alec said. "You could have been killed. Can you breathe all right?"

"My head," she said, her hand moving to the top of it.

"Should I call a medic?" he asked Denny. "Or drive her to a medical facility?"

"With all this snow, how would you get her there?" Denny asked.

"I could give it a try," Alec said.

"Good luck with that." Denny felt annoyance roiling inside of her.

"And how about you?" Denny asked Amanda. "Your mother would kill me if anything happened to you." She was trying to keep her voice uplifted while she kept herself from crying. When it came down to it, Denny held few people more precious than Amanda, who loved her unconditionally.

Mrs. Ross stepped outside wearing a long coat. "Everyone all right?"

"Yes, but let's get these ladies inside." Alec slid his arm around Lydia's shoulder. "Let me grab your hat." He plucked Lydia's knit beanie out of the snow, gave it a shake, and then crammed it in his pocket.

133

"But I want to play in the snow," Amanda said. "What if this turns to rain and I miss my chance to make a snow angel and build a snowman?"

The wind picked up, tossing the snow and biting into Denny's cheeks. "It still feels below freezing to me." She turned to Alec, but he was already trudging toward the hotel with his arm supporting Lydia and not giving Denny a second look to assess her safety.

"Let's get you back inside for hot chocolate," Denny said to Amanda. Denny didn't even know how to make hot chocolate unless it came from a box, but it didn't look as though Lydia would be cooking anymore this morning. She was milking this snowfall for all it was worth. Not fair, Denny reminded herself, Lydia had been knocked off her feet by the snow. Denny needed to show compassion. But she felt resentment clawing into her. She wished she was home and welcoming the first customers to her bookshop, then she remembered she would soon be out of business. She was going bankrupt. And her parents were dead. How could she forget her dismal situation for these temporary distractions?

After ten minutes Denny coerced Amanda into coming back into the hotel with the promise of something yummy. In front of the hearth, Alec fussed over Lydia, who was sitting in an overstuffed chair. Denny had to wonder. Like her father, she had never shown pain and rarely cried. But she felt like sobbing right now.

"I'm going to dash into the kitchen and grab some coffee," Denny told Amanda. "And I'll see about getting you hot chocolate."

A few patrons sat at tables; their voices subdued. Surely Alec had seen her enter the building, as did Lydia, who said nothing about Amanda's well-being. Lifting her chin, Denny entered the kitchen, where much to her surprise she found Maureen at the helm.

"Don't worry about Amanda; she seems to be fine," Denny said.

Maureen was fully dressed and wore a white apron. "What happened? Did I miss something?"

"Snow slid off the roof is all. Nothing to worry about. Amanda's okay." She neared Maureen and noticed a blush of color in her cheeks. "What goes on?" Denny asked.

"When I ordered breakfast to the room, I was told that the hotel had no cook. Which surprised me because I thought Lydia was cooking this morning. You know me. I came down to investigate and to see if I could help." She smirked. "When I got down here, I apologized profusely for last night's smoke fiasco. Mrs. Ross promptly told me I was forgiven if I would help with breakfast and lunch." She shrugged. "I've been having so much fun that I forgot to make breakfast for myself. You want anything?"

"Sure, I'm starving. And Amanda would like some hot chocolate and a treat if you can think of one."

"I'll whip up some hot chocolate the way Amanda likes it." Maureen chortled. "Amanda claims Lydia makes better hot chocolate than I do even though Lydia's using my recipe."

"Well, since you're in the mood to cook, I would love a cheese omelet."

"One hot chocolate and a cheese omelet coming right up. Would you like toast with that?"

"Yes, please." Denny hadn't seen her older sister so full of vitality in years. She watched Maureen prepare the hot chocolate and pour it into a mug with an abundance of mini marshmallows. "Allow me." Denny took hold of the handle.

"Wait, I have buttered toast." Maureen handed her a plate. She seemed back to her old self.

Denny brought the hot chocolate and toast to the table for Amanda.

"I thought only Lydia knew how to make hot chocolate," Amanda said.

"Seriously? Your mother said she taught Lydia."

Denny's mind circled back to the puppies in the basement, but she did not want to disturb Princess, who needed her rest.

Chapter 36

Maureen's heart was beating double-time—in a good way—and her brain was whirring with new ideas. She had not heard from the TV network but assumed her show had been snuffed. If the network executives could only see her now. She would have the last laugh. When she got back to the room, she would call her attorney to make sure she wasn't violating any contractual agreements by writing a cookbook. A lawsuit wouldn't help anyone. James would throw a conniption. What if Amanda was correct in her allegations about James's infidelity? Would her husband have the gall to cheat on her after the death of her parents? For all she knew, he had been unfaithful to her their whole marriage.

While in the kitchen preparing Denny's omelet, beating the eggs to a light and fluffy froth, Maureen planned her new cookbook, which would be a smash, a *New York Times* bestseller. She loved the Scottish theme. Her mind filled with ideas. When the snow let up, she would shower, dress, and look her best, then ask the obnoxious reporter to come back again. Someone would know the name of his employer. The *Gazette* would have the pleasure of announcing her new venture. Literary agents had approached her for years. All she needed to do was choose one and call their office.

Maureen toyed with the idea of extending their trip another month right here on the Isle of Skye. Then when home, after the book's release, she'd have a book signing in the Big Apple. She'd hire a publicist to help launch her new career.

She selected a mélange of cheeses from the refrigerator and grated several, then she chopped green onions. She was out to impress her little sister, which brought a smile to Maureen's face. Yet she had a nagging feeling someone was out to ruin her. Someone who wanted her spot on the TV show. They could have it. Maureen realized she couldn't care less. Whoever it was could not replace the one and only Maureen Cook, who would emerge victorious. If only her parents were here to encourage her. Stop, she told herself. She must not return to that swamp of despair. She had money in the bank, her daughter, and talent galore.

Then a spectacular thought came to mind. She could direct and produce her own TV show, filmed right in her home's kitchen. It had been updated last year and had all the amenities she'd need. Her followers would adore it. She had learned enough over the years to swing it. She'd switch to another network that had been begging her for years. Of course, she'd demand a bonus... Hold on, as the boss, she could have anything she wanted—just like Martha Stewart.

She cut into the butter and then slipped a small yellow cube into her warming pan, producing a sizzle. She poured the eggs atop the butter and sprinkled on the grated cheese. How she adored cooking.

She would miss the crew she'd grown so close to such as the cameramen, lighting experts, and the magical makeup and wardrobe gurus—who might jump at the chance of following her on her new venture. She imagined herself taking the recipes out of her new cooking book and selling thousands of copies each week.

Another bonus: she would be home every afternoon when Amanda returned from school. In the blink of an eye, her daughter would be headed off to college. Maureen hoped, anyway. Amanda didn't seem to have much interest in school, but Maureen would at least be there when her daughter got home from school. And Maureen couldn't count on Lydia working for her forever. Another six months at the most was what Lydia had promised.

Maureen admired her lovely omelet, browned just the way she knew Denny liked it. She looked around for a clean and attractive plate and found one with a pink floral rim. She wondered what she would use for embellishment but remembered Denny wouldn't care and hated parsley. Oh dear, Maureen had forgotten to put in the toast. Cooking in this foreign kitchen had thrown her off her game, but she recovered when she noticed a bag of bread. She slid a couple of slices in the toaster, then headed into the dining room.

"One cheese omelet." Maureen placed it before Denny. "What condiment would you like with your toast?" Maureen asked.

"More toast? I shouldn't but since you ask." Denny patted her flat tummy. "Honey, strawberry and raspberry jams, and marmalade are already on the table."

"Perfect." Maureen scanned the dining room looking for Lydia. Maureen finally located her at a table with Alec. Maureen turned to speak to her sister. "What on earth do Lydia and Alec have to talk about? Why isn't she looking after Amanda?"

"In all fairness, that block of snow that fell off the roof knocked Lydia unconscious for a moment." Denny turned to watch them too. "Do I think she's taking advantage of the situation? Sure looks like it. Men can be so dumb when it comes to the guiles of women."

Maureen thought of her husband and couldn't disagree. But she didn't want to make a snide comment about James.

Chapter 37

Lydia felt duplicitous, but she was thoroughly enjoying Alec's attention. Her parents would be outraged.

"Tell me more about yourself," Alec said to her.

"Not much to tell." Lydia had been taught since she was a young child never to lie, and yet the words came out easily. She was becoming a master of deceit. "You must already know that I'm Amanda's nanny."

He waited.

"And I do housecleaning. When needed. The Cooks' house doesn't get very dirty, other than Amanda's messy room." She felt her lids sliding shut. "I'm so tired."

Mrs. Ross came over with the coffee carafe and poured Alec a cup. "If she lost consciousness, then she needs to stay awake," she said. "I read about head injuries just last week."

Lydia felt like falling asleep and letting her head slump against the table.

Mrs. Ross shook her shoulder. "Hey there, lassie, wake up."

"But I'm so tired." Lydia yawned.

Mrs. Ross spoke to Alec. "Keep her talking."

"I want to hear about you," Alec said to Lydia as he watched Mrs. Ross disappear into the kitchen. "Where are you from."

"Why do you want to know so much?" Lydia asked. "If you knew how evil I am, you wouldn't like me. Not even as a friend."

"I doubt that very much." His voice reflected humor. "Did you kill someone or what?"

The burden of holding in her secrets was too much. Suddenly she found herself spewing out the truth. "I've broken the teachings of the *Ordnung*—the laws Amish must obey—and the teachings of the Bible."

"What could be so bad?"

She felt heat crawling up her neck and into her cheeks. "I'm a liar and a thief. And I pay money to a man who's blackmailing me."

"Who is it? What for?"

"A man caught me stealing shoes at his store, and he's been blackmailing me ever since." She shivered at the miscreant's alternative to money.

"Blackmail is against the law. In some ways, it's worse than theft."

"Maybe so but I am guilty. And he will hold this over me for the rest of my life." She forced herself through the layers of consciousness until she found Alec's hazel eyes. "Perhaps I could move here and work at this hotel as a cook or a waitress and never go home."

"I've found that running away from the truth is never the answer."

She waited for him to chastise her. She deserved punishment, even if it meant punishing herself.

"I was falsely accused of cheating on a test in college and was expelled," he said. "I was innocent, but my test disappeared. I didn't try hard enough to rid myself of the stain of guilt. As a result, my father disowned me. I'm not even allowed inside our ancestral castle."

"What? Your family owns a castle?"

"Yes." He nodded without enthusiasm. "I am the first of Clan MacLeod for five hundred years to be unwelcome there."

"I sure wish I could see it." Lydia was fully awake now.

"I wish you could too. It's the oldest continuously inhabited castle in Scotland. It's open to the public to pay property taxes. And my parents are in London." He glanced to the window. "But we're staying put with all this snow."

Lydia yawned again, and her eyes slid closed.

"Promise me you'll stay awake." He sent her a grin. "Or I'll ask Amanda to fetch a handful of snow to smear in your face."

"You wouldn't dare." She giggled. "Would you?"

Chapter 38

"I don't believe it," Denny muttered while Amanda was looking out the window at the onslaught of snow. "That little vixen is out to steal Alec's heart," she told Maureen when Maureen took a seat next to her.

"You can't deny she's very sweet and pretty," Maureen said. "I've caught James staring at her more than once."

Denny assessed her older sister's face. "She's no better looking than you are."

"Yeah, right. And ten years younger."

"Age isn't everything."

"If you say so."

Denny had already fed Princess and checked on the puppies. Rosie in particular. Denny was amazed at how full of love her heart felt when she saw little Rosie. This must be what it was like to fall in love. She realized she hadn't loved any of her former boyfriends. She looked across the room at Alec and had to admit she was attracted to him. But he, apparently, had no interest in her. He was eating up Lydia's flirtatious nature. She wished she could hear what they were talking about. Their faces changed from seriousness to levity.

"I'd better get back in the kitchen," Maureen said to Denny. "I should be taking photos. May I borrow your phone?"

As Denny handed the phone to Maureen, it rang. Denny recognized the ring tone as belonging to Agnes from her bookstore.

"I can't come to work today," Agnes said. "I'm sick. Just a

head cold, but I can't go to work like this." She sneezed, then coughed.

"Is there someone who can fill in for you?" Denny already knew the answer was no.

"Sorry, all my friends have jobs or little kids to take care of." Agnes sneezed.

Denny should hop on the next jet home but wouldn't. "Don't worry about it," she told Agnes. Denny pictured her cozy little bookstore dark and devoid of customers. Hardly anyone came in there, so what was the big deal? She hated to admit that her father had been right. "Like flushing money down the toilet," he'd told her more than once.

Denny felt devastated that her parents had died in debt. She couldn't have helped them, but maybe Maureen would have been able to, although she doubted James would cough up a penny for their parents.

Her hunch was their father had invested in a startup company that flopped. Put all his eggs in one basket, as they say.

No use wallowing in remorse over her parents. She had problems enough right where she was in the present. She glanced across the room and tried to get Alec's attention, but he was fixated on speaking to Lydia.

"Well?" Maureen asked. "May I use your phone? I want to take pictures of my breakfast dishes as I prepare them."

"Yes, although my phone is ancient, and I think yours has a much better camera on it—doesn't it."

"You're right. I'll dash upstairs and get it if you'll keep an eye on Amanda. I don't want her going outside again. Too dangerous."

"Sure, Sis." Denny found herself standing but couldn't recall getting up. She plopped down on a chair and decided to be content. *Contentment* and *gratitude* would be her words for the day—if she could swing it.

Alec escorted Lydia to the table. "According to Mrs. Ross, if Lydia has a head concussion, she should not fall asleep. I was having a hard time entertaining her." They both sat across the table from Denny. Lydia did look dazed, but Denny didn't buy it. Amanda landed next to Lydia and started chattering about playing outside again.

"Sorry, sweetie, but I promised your mother I'd keep you inside," Denny said, already fretting about her bookstore again. She knew she'd feel better if she could get out and purchase more merchandise. Yet she'd go further into debt. But she hated to lose the one job she had enjoyed. Her own little bookshop. She remembered opening night and the excitement she'd felt. Her mother had attended the festive evening, but her father had stayed home with some excuse Denny didn't believe. And yet Denny missed him beyond words. She missed both of her parents, for different reasons.

Twenty minutes later Maureen descended the stairs a changed woman. She'd showered and coiffed her hair into a French roll. And she wore a snazzy fuchsia-colored dress that Denny had never seen before. And matching three-inch heels. Denny was happy to see her sister feeling her old self but had to wonder how she planned to cook dressed that way. Was she expecting a camera crew?

Alec got to his feet as she neared the table. "You look very nice, Mrs. Cook," he said.

"Please call me Maureen."

"I agree," Denny said. "You look gorgeous."

"Are you going to work?" Amanda asked her.

"Not exactly." Maureen spoke to Denny. "May I impose on you for a few minutes to take pictures of me?"

Denny rolled her eyes. "Sure, no trouble," she said. "Call me when you need me."

"In other words, you're not coming out to play with me in the snow?" Amanda said, her face reddening as it often did before a tantrum. Denny had witnessed her tantrums since Amanda was a three-year-old.

Denny would ignore her. Dad would do the same thing. He would not tolerate bad behavior.

"Your mother told me not to let you outside again."

Amanda's face screwed up. "I thought you liked me."

"I do, very much. But you saw what happened. The snow is sliding off the roof of the building. It could have killed you." Denny knew she was being a drama queen, but she needed to make her point and stay firm. Lydia seemed to have no desire to help with Amanda's behavior, which irked Denny. Lydia was being paid to take care of the girl, plus an all-expense-paid trip to Scotland. Not that Denny wasn't the recipient of a free trip here too. She needed to thank Maureen, but now was not the time. She would go into the kitchen to be Maureen's assistant. And Denny was a pretty good photographer when it came down to it.

But for now, she would sit with Alec and Lydia. As she looked at Alec across the table, she felt a purr of attraction. He glanced up at that moment, and their eyes met. Oh yeah, she liked this guy, which was totally ridiculous. Alec lived in another country. She didn't even know how long she had to live—literally. She would enjoy him for as long as she was here. A whirlwind romance like those in the movies. She remembered her father's words: it takes two to tango. Her shoulders slumped. No one tangoed anymore, and she was a party of one.

The hotel's front door opened with such force that it rattled on its hinges. A burly redheaded man wearing knee-high boots and what appeared to be a hunting jacket strode in.

"Here's Gordon MacDonald, the hotel's sole proprietor." Alec stood and extended his arm to shake the man's hand. "Good morning, Gordon."

"What in heaven's name is going on?" His ruddy face radiated anger. "Where is everyone?"

Denny had seen worse and was not afraid to speak. She recalled how she'd been the only one who would stand up to their father. "Good morning, I'm Denny—" She decided to be prudent and not mention her last name since Campbells were not welcome on Skye. She put out her hand, but the hulk of a man did not shake it. She was a paying customer, and her sister was cooking in the kitchen. How dare he treat her like a nobody?

He tugged on his shaggy red beard.

"Who are you?" he asked her.

"A paying customer." She looked around the dining room. "One of the few who stayed when the electricity and heat went out last night. And my sister is cooking in the kitchen."

"Without my permission?"

Denny folded her arms across her chest and glared back at him. "She is a world-famous chef, and you're lucky to have her." Denny was not afraid of anyone. At least she wouldn't let him know she was. In the depths of her mind, she heard her dad singing, "The Campbells are coming, hurrah, hurrah!"

At that moment, Maureen strolled out of the kitchen in all her glory. Gordon MacDonald was obviously wowed by her radiance. How could he not be? Her hips swaying, Maureen looked ravishing and confident in her fuchsia calf-length gown.

"Meet my sister, Maureen," Denny said.

Chapter 39

"Who have we here?" Maureen asked, her lips wearing glossy fuchsia lipstick.

"Uh... I'm Gordon MacDonald." The man stuck out a burley hand to shake hers.

She paused for a moment until he'd dried his hand off on his slacks, and then she shook his. "I'm Maureen Cook, and I've decided to write a cookbook, which will feature your hotel, if you don't mind."

When he didn't respond, she added, "Next time you're on your computer, Google me to see my credentials. Or hop on YouTube. In the meantime, my sister is going to take some photos of me preparing breakfast in your kitchen. If you don't mind. If you do, I'll simply go somewhere else where I will be welcomed." Maureen knew her name would pop up hundreds of times on the internet. Not to mention YouTube. She was world-famous, she told herself. She hadn't been fired yet.

"Do you advertise with the *Gazette*?" she asked Gordon. "A reporter was in here last night taking pictures of me. Would you please contact him and see if he can get down here again with a photographer?"

Gordon stood mesmerized. "That might have to wait for the snow to let up."

"You know best." Maureen had barely been able to zip up her dress an hour ago, and her toes pinched in these high heels. Was it possible to gain weight in such a short time? She'd have to keep an eye on her calorie count.

Mrs. Ross hovered in the distance. "Get a reporter down here," Gordon said to her. "Tell him Mrs. Cook needs a cameraman too." Gordon's face transformed into one of elation; he was no longer a brute. "Anything else we can get you?" he asked Maureen. "Anything at all?"

"I just had a stupendous idea," she said. "You may not be aware of it, but you have honeymooners staying at the hotel. In their honor, I'll prepare something extra special. And photograph it for the press. Of course, we will mention this hotel and how much we love it." Maureen batted her eyes. She liked the rough-and-tumble appearance of this bearded man, and she could tell he appreciated her looks. She caught him glancing down at her ankles. She was glad she'd gone the extra mile to look good. Not that she'd come on this trip to flirt with a stranger. But what could it hurt? Her husband never complimented her.

"In the meantime, my sister will do the honors with my phone. Not a perfect camera but pretty darn good."

"Absolutely." Denny popped to her feet. "Ready and willing."

Maureen had always thought that Denny was better looking than she was. Slim and trim and agile, Denny didn't need makeup to look beautiful. Alec's eyes followed her younger sister. Maureen could tell he was entranced. And what man wouldn't be?

"Say, Gordon, hadn't you better fix the hole in your roof?" Denny asked him as if they were old friends.

He glared at her.

"All in good time," Maureen said. "I'm sure Gordon knows what needs to be taken care of first."

Alec stood. "When you're ready, I'd be happy to run upstairs with you, sir. Being unable to drive these lovely ladies around the island, I find myself idle."

"Then come outside and play with me," Amanda said, stomping her feet. "And Lydia too."

Maureen figured her daughter was holding in a powder-keg of frustration. It must be boring without any other kids her age to hang out with. But Maureen was determined to keep Amanda inside.

Kate Lloyd

"Dearest daughter, that falling snow from the rooftop banged Lydia's head and knocked her out for a moment or two. Long enough to be of worry. I think Mrs. Ross's idea about keeping Lydia awake is the best plan." Maureen waited for a meltdown, but so far Amanda was keeping her cool.

"She hates me," Amanda said. "All of you do."

"Nothing could be further from the truth," Denny said.

"Aunt Denny, I know you love me."

"We all do," Maureen said. "Maybe Mr. MacDonald will let you go down and see the new puppies."

"I don't know, I don't want anything to upset Princess." Gordon's gaze never left Maureen. "I should go down there right now to make sure she and her new wee family are doing well. Would you like to join me, Maureen?"

"Yes, I would." Maureen turned to Amanda. "You may come with me only if you're on your best behavior and keep your distance. Understand?"

Amanda's demeanor changed to one of happiness. "Yes, I'll be on my absolute best behavior."

"And that means using your indoor voice."

"I'll make sure she does," Denny said.

"I don't know," Gordon said.

Maureen reminded herself that she was used to handling belligerent men. She hated to admit she was conniving, one reason she'd climbed so high.

She slipped her arm through the bend of Gordon's elbow. "We will all be very quiet," she told him.

Denny sprang to her feet. "I'll go with you. Princess knows me well."

"How is that?" Gordon asked.

"I've been feeding her and bringing her fresh water. I watched her whelp per puppies and have chosen the one I want."

"I will not be selling any of them." Gordon's voice turned belligerent. "And certainly not give one away."

Maureen watched Denny's smile droop. But fortunately, she

148

pursed her lips and said nothing. Maureen remembered Denny's many go-rounds with their father, who had wanted her to become a lawyer. Maureen had often thought Denny could be an attorney, the way she carried on is if she were in a court room.

Maureen looked up to Gordon's ruggedly handsome face and said, "Did I mention we might be staying here for another month? If you have the room, that is."

"We'll make the room." He stopped walking and gazed down at her. "I am the boss around here."

"I know. You make all the final decisions." After being married to James for almost fifteen years, Maureen knew how to act her submissive self when in fact she didn't feel it. She was superior to James in many ways. Her mother had pointed this out to Maureen often.

Maureen was pleased when she entered the kitchen and found it neat and tidy. Molly must have come in here while Maureen was showering. Maureen was used to working on the set, where people came behind her and cleared all her messes away. Those days were over because Maureen must start acting like a nobody until she planted her feet well under her. Until she had snagged Gordon's admiration. Piece of cake, she told herself.

Gordon led the way to the basement. Fair enough, Maureen thought. Placing a finger on her lips to shush everyone, she turned behind her and saw Denny, Lydia, and Amanda. Alec followed behind them. As Gordon put out his hand to Princess, she growled and bared her front teeth at him.

He withdrew his hand. "What's this?" he asked the room at large. "Who has turned my Princess against me?"

No one dared to say a word. At least that's what Maureen surmised. But then Denny moved closer and stroked the puppies, her fingertips lingering on Rosie.

"How dare you?" Gordan asked her.

"Denny has always loved dogs," Maureen said, "and they've loved her. But our father would never let her have one."

"But all that's about to change," Denny said. "If you'll sell me Rosie."

149

"My answer is an emphatic no." Gordan seemed to grow in stature. "Are you deaf?"

Maureen saw the hurt in Denny's eyes. She seemed to be holding in tears. But couldn't her sister find a cairn terrier puppy when she got home? Shouldn't she be worried about her bookstore? Maureen reminded herself that she herself had been out of sorts ever since their parents had died. Her priorities had been out of whack, living in a world where nothing made sense.

For one thing Maureen wondered if she loved James anymore. He was the last person she turned to for advice or encouragement. Why hadn't he called her to at least ask how Amanda was doing? Not that Amanda had asked to speak to her dad. Their family was two-dimensional instead of three. Flat. Almost nonexistent.

Alec's voice shattered the silence. "Gordon, you want my assistance in the attic?"

"'Tis a miserable day." Gordon stood to face Alec but found Maureen instead. He couldn't help but grin at her. Or so it seemed to Maureen. "Yes, I'd gladly take your help," Gordon said. "It's been years since I've been up there. I shudder to think of what has been ruined."

"It's a mess all right, but Denny saved Bonnie Prince Charlie's cap."

"Where is it now?" Gordon glowered at Denny, but she smiled back at him.

"I gave it to Mrs. Ross to put somewhere safe," she said. "I assume she's trustworthy."

"Yes, she is," Gordon said. "I suppose I must thank you for that. But no time for pleasantries. Alec, I'm ready when you are."

"Which I am right now." Alec turned and placed his foot on the first step. A moment later the two men lumbered up the stairs with Lydia on their heels. Maureen was glad to have that altercation deflated but sad to see Gordon leave. Was it just her imagination or had he really found her attractive? She supposed she shouldn't care, but she did.

150

Chapter 40

Lydia followed Alec and Gordon up to the attic. She figured she could be of assistance and get a chance to be alone with Alec. She had seen many a water leak in the house's, barn's or storage shed's roof and was confident she could help them. If they'd let her.

Gordon groaned when he saw the water dripping in through the roof's hole. "How will I get repairmen on a day like today?" he asked Alec. "Do you know anyone?"

"I do have friends who are roofers but persuading them up there today will be a challenge. Too dangerous." Alec examined a spot where water was leaking. "Lydia might have the best idea in putting metal containers under the damaged spots where it's leaking until you can get professionals here."

Lydia was happy to hear Alec speak her name, as if he were singing a melody.

She raised a timid hand and said, "Hello, I'm Lydia," but Gordon paid her no heed. Back at home, he would have at least acknowledged her existence. She missed her parents' community even with its never-ending chores.

She spoke to Alec. "What would you like me to do?"

"How about running downstairs and seeing if you can find any empty buckets. I doubt you're strong enough to carry this water down."

"I'm pretty strong," she said and then felt embarrassed for bragging. But water couldn't weigh any more than milk. She attempted to lift a metal container of water but found it too heavy.

"Never mind. I'll run that downstairs and empty it," Alec said.

Lydia did not want to be left alone with Gordon, but she said, "Danke—I mean thank you. In the meantime, I'll find more metal containers." But when she looked around, she noticed Gordon staring at her with a steady gaze as if sizing her up.

"I'll empty one too." Gordon grasped another container filled with water and splashed some on his leg. He let out what must be a Scottish expletive and then followed Alec down the stairs. Lydia could see that both men were twice as strong as she was. Still, there must be something she could do. She located one more metal container crammed with silverware and dumped the contents onto the floor. An ornate silver goblet rolled to her feet. So pretty. Lydia was seized with the desire to stuff it in a pocket. No one would be the wiser. But she heard her father's voice in her ear, and she was filled with shame for even considering stealing again. She imagined Gordon pressing charges and having her incarcerated. She'd never go anywhere if she were in a Scottish jail. And anyway, stealing others' property was against the law because it was wrong. What was she thinking? Hadn't she promised herself she would never steal anything ever again?

She heard men's voice chatting and heavy footsteps on the stairs. Moments later she saw Alec and Gordon, each carrying two empty buckets by their handles.

"Ach, I'm sorry to leave such a mess." Lydia looked down at the silverware and the goblet that she had coveted on the floor. "I didn't know where to put these items." A half-truth but at least she hadn't stolen anything. Would temptation always haunt her?

"No matter," Gordon said. "Leave everything where it is. That hodgepodge needs to be sorted through anyway. One of my employees can do that later tomorrow or next week. After the snow lets up. And melts." For the first time, he studied her face as if assessing her. Could he tell just by looking at her that she was being pulled in two directions—between good and evil? Maybe everyone was. But she was determined to walk the straight and narrow, as her dat would say. To follow the teachings of the Bible and the Ordnung.

She stooped down and gathered up flatware, transferred it into a cardboard box. As she added the goblet, she gave it one last looking over. It needed to be polished, a chore she would gladly do. In so many ways, life was easier back in her Amish home where someone would be looking over her shoulder and steering her on the right course.

Chapter 41

Denny was glad to know that Gordon, a harsh man, was upstairs. She had to wonder if Alec had led him away to avoid conflict. In any case, Denny was happy to have Gordon gone so she could stroke her little Rosie for a moment. As she did, her mind explored the avenues of leaving Skye and returning home to her failing bookstore and the reality of her illness. She both wanted to return home and to stay here. She felt tugged in both directions. Not to mention Alec, the first man she'd found herself truly attracted to in years.

She cut her time with Rosie short in case Gordon returned. Did her older sister really have an attraction for him? How weird was that? Denny supposed no more peculiar than her falling for Alec—she knew she had—a man who lived on the other side of the Atlantic Ocean. She didn't even know if he liked dogs or books. Or if he was smitten with Lydia or Molly.

When she reached the kitchen, she found her sister tying on an apron—cinching it tightly around her waist. Denny reminded herself that Maureen hadn't even met Gordon when she put on that curvaceous fuchsia dress. She couldn't recall seeing her older sister in such high heels nor swishing around as she had earlier. But her flirtatious mannerisms had certainly been for his attention once they'd met. Denny had never seen Maureen so aflutter. Not since high school when the captain of the football team asked her out to the homecoming dance. Not fair. Maureen was over the moon when James pursued her in college and then proposed almost immediately. Denny replayed Maureen and her mother

154

planning the opulent wedding and sit-down dinner for three hundred guests after the church ceremony in record time. An event worthy of the cover of a magazine for brides. Is that when her parents went into debt, a truth that still sent Denny reeling?

Denny felt as if she were shrinking while thoughts about her uncertain future gyrated through her brain. If she did get married, who would walk her down the aisle and give her away? Who would pay for the wedding? Not to mention her gown. And the food—Denny would be happy with a buffet and fold-up chairs.

Whom was she kidding? She had no groom. She had no future. She'd be happy with a justice of the peace if only someone like Alec loved her. She felt like a crumb swirling down the drain. Was life even worth living?

Whoa, now was not the time to wallow in self-pity. Get a grip, she told herself.

She wandered into the dining room and saw that several people were seated at tables. Denny rushed into the kitchen. "Hungry customers," she said to her sister.

Maureen handed her an order pad. "Find out what they want, please."

Denny might as well keep busy. "Okay, will do." Minutes later she took orders from the two couples and then returned to Maureen. "Do you know how to make this stuff?"

Maureen pulled fresh biscuits from the oven. "Yes. A piece of cake."

Denny inhaled the tantalizing aromas. "Even the smoked kippers?"

"'Fake it 'til you bake it' is my motto." Maureen winked at her. "Anything I can't concoct, you can tell them the ingredients went bad when the electricity went out."

Gordon sauntered into the kitchen and stood watching Maureen. He inhaled through his nostrils. "Smells good," he said. "You're an angel."

"Why thank you, kind sir." Maureen's face radiated happiness.

"If they give you a bad time, tell them it's on the house," Gordon said to Denny. "Meaning no charge."

"Sorry." Molly tottered into the kitchen looking groggy. "I fell asleep." She flushed water into the kettle. "We'll be needing hot water for tea."

"I should have thought of that." Working in a kitchen was a new terrain to Denny. She admired her sister's proficiency. "In the meantime, I'll offer them coffee." Denny took hold of the coffee carafe's handle. If she knew nothing else, she could plaster on a phony smile when her insides felt like melting Jell-O. An American couple who'd walked here from a nearby hotel was grateful for the coffee. The other couple, visiting from London, said they preferred tea. "Coming right up," Denny said.

Denny and Molly worked in tandem keeping those two couples satisfied, but what would happen if more hungry people arrived? Each time Denny stepped into the kitchen she heard Maureen singing or humming, "Speed, bonnie boat, like a bird on the wing. Onward, the sailors cry," as she prepared oatmeal and egg dishes, pan-fried sausages, and chatted with Gordon, who seemed captivated with her.

Denny pulled out Maureen's cell phone and took as many photos as she could between delivering orders and clearing away plates.

"Sis, Amanda could help you," Maureen said." It wouldn't hurt her to pull her own weight."

"Maybe Lydia could pitch in. She should be helping too, right? I assume you're paying her."

"Where is she?" Maureen asked.

"In the dining room somewhere, I think." Denny poked her head out of the kitchen. "She and Amanda must have scampered upstairs together."

"Please tell me they wouldn't go outside—would they?" Maureen asked.

"I doubt it after what they went through. And the snow is still coming down. Unbelievable." Denny gazed out the window and saw two men with shovels. "I'll run upstairs and check in our room."

"Thanks, otherwise I'll be worried sick." Maureen set a fry pan on the stove top. "I've got cooking to do." She appeared in her element, anything but worried.

"Happy to help. I'll find her. She's probably with Lydia." Denny hurried up the stairs to their room and opened the door to find Lydia dozing atop her bed. She lifted her head when the door opened.

"Do you know where Amanda is?" Denny asked.

"*Nee*—no idea. I thought she was with you." Lydia pushed herself to a sitting position.

"Never mind, I'll find her." Denny checked in Maureen's room and found it empty, then went back for her jacket and hat. Planning to head outside to look for Amanda, Denny wrestled on her jacket and hat and trotted down the stairs too fast and ran into Alec, who wrapped his arms around Denny to stabilize her. Their faces were only inches apart. She had a crazy notion to kiss him, and he seemed to be thinking the same thing. Neither moved for a minute as she breathed in the intoxicating aromas of his breath and aftershave.

The world seemed to stop revolving, but Denny's thoughts zigzagged through the stratosphere. She reminded herself she barely knew Alec. He had never shown her much attention. Although he'd been very helpful with Rosie. He had been helpful in the attic. And he seemed to get along well with Gordon, but what did that have to do with anything?

"Have you seen Amanda?" she finally asked—the last thing on her mind when it should be her priority.

"I saw Lydia in the attic a while ago, but Amanda wasn't with her." Alec's hand stayed anchored at her waist. "Should we check for Amanda outside?"

Denny bristled with irritation, but she kept her face from grimacing. "Lydia was up in the attic with you?"

"Yes, but that was half an hour ago." He glanced out the

window. "I thought you were looking for your sister's daughter, Amanda."

"Yes, I am. That little scamp must be outside somewhere playing in the snow."

She and Alec bundled up and stepped out into the storm. A blast of freezing air slapped Denny's face. Denny took Alec's elbow. They walked around the hotel, passed the two men shoveling snow. A lost cause because the snow accumulated again wherever they'd cleared. Denny saw several kids embroiled in a snowball fight, but none were Amanda.

"Do you think she might've walked to Portree?" Alec asked Denny.

"I doubt it, although I suppose she could have accepted a ride. I wouldn't put it past her to hitchhike." Denny cringed at the thought of Amanda getting in a car with a stranger.

"Not many vehicles on the road, but it's possible."

"Don't you have any snowplows?" Denny asked, feeling cranky.

"No. It rarely snows on Skye. I've never seen so much snow. On the higher elevations, that's a whole different story." Alec approached the kids throwing snowballs and spoke to them for several minutes. He returned to Denny and said, "They said a car stopped for a few minutes, but they couldn't tell if anyone got in. Then it continued on down the road, they think toward Portree. But they're not sure."

Denny felt heat radiating from under her collar. She was tempted to tromp over there herself and ask them, but the kids were traveling in a pack away from them. She'd never catch up.

Alec and Denny circled back once more around the hotel, twice to make sure, and then finally toddled into the kitchen where they found Maureen serving up a sumptuous breakfast to Gordan.

"I assume you found her," Maureen said.

"Not yet." Denny was tempted to describe Lydia's lazing on her bed.

"Maybe she's downstairs with the pups," Alec said.

Denny took the excuse to descend the stairs to see Rosie, then came back up again. She saw fear in Maureen's eyes when Denny said, "Nope, Amanda's not there."

"Better call the police," Maureen said. "She might have been kidnapped."

"I can hear their questions now," Gordon said. "She's been missing for only an hour."

Maureen tore off her apron, dropped it on a counter. "I've got to find her."

"Does she have a history of running away?" Alec asked.

"No, but she's my daughter."

"I'll drop everything and look for her," Gordon said. "No one knows this island better than I do. And I'll call everyone I know, which includes most of the business owners in Portree. But I'm guessing they're not open today."

"Thank you so much." Maureen grasped his forearm.

Denny wanted to point out that he hadn't done anything for Maureen yet except flirt. Denny was determined to find Amanda. "If she'd been kidnapped, wouldn't someone have called asking for ransom money?" She watched Maureen's face blanche.

"Just because no one has called demanding ransom money doesn't mean she hasn't been abducted," Maureen said.

"Between Gordon and me, we can put out the red alert to everyone on the island," Alec said. "And let's look for her. You up for it, Gordon?"

"As soon as the hotel is back to running." Gordon glanced Maureen's way, and she frowned. "On second thought, maybe I had better go with you," Gordon said. "What would you like, Maureen?"

Denny answered for her sister. "She wants her daughter back."

"I have an idea," Gordon said. "We split up instead of running all around like chickens with their heads cut off."

Denny did not appreciate his glib attitude. She saw nothing amusing in the situation.

159

"No one has been kidnapped on Skye for over one hundred years," Gordon said. "Not to my knowledge."

Denny hoped he was speaking the truth. But she also knew the world was full of evil people.

Chapter 42

"Wait a minute," Maureen said to Gordon. "How did you get here?"

"In my Range Rover. I'm used to driving over rough terrain."

"Are you leaving? If so, I want to go with you."

"Dressed like that? Not that you don't look bonnie in that dress."

"Give me five minutes to change my clothes." Maureen dreaded putting on slacks and a turtleneck. She knew she looked fetching in this dress, but suddenly her looks, her future book, and her career seemed meaningless in comparison with her daughter's safety. Amanda was probably hiding upstairs in a closet or pulling a prank, her usual routine. Because the girl would do anything for attention. Maureen wondered why that was, but now was not the time to ponder her daughter's personality quirks.

Maureen turned to Denny. "Are you sure she isn't hiding somewhere in this hotel?" she asked.

"I haven't looked in every single room, if that's what you're asking." Denny glanced to Alec. "Want to have one more look in this place?" she asked him.

"Sure, if someone will give me the master keys." Alec put out a hand to Gordon, who reluctantly gave him a ring of keys. "But let's face it, how would Amanda get into those rooms without a key?"

"Good question," Gordon said. "Have you already checked everywhere she could go without a key?"

"As far as I know," Alec said. "And I can't imagine she's hiding outside because it's biting cold."

Every head pivoted toward Maureen, who turned off the stovetop, set the frypan aside. All those days and nights she'd been away from her daughter so that she could be a star, so that she could be in the limelight. She felt like a fool.

"If she's hiding somewhere in the hotel, she will be in so much trouble." Maureen's gut told her that Amanda was not anywhere in this building. Maureen knew that she indulged Amanda. Maureen had turned her into a poor little spoiled brat.

Maureen tore off the apron and set it aside. She kicked off her heels, then she sprinted up the stairs and into her room, where she hoped to find Amanda. But no such luck. She wriggled out of her dress, then put on slacks and a turtleneck sweater and her jacket.

Gordon shook his head when he saw her. "Hold on." He reached into a closet and extracted a fleece-lined rain jacket. "You'd better wear this too. And these Wellies." He brought out a pair of tall rubber boots. "This closet is where we put all the items left behind by guests."

Maureen stepped into the boots and wrestled into the jacket. She must look like a goof, but she didn't care. "Thank you."

"Now all you need is a hat." Gordon reached into the closet and pulled out a baseball cap with earflaps.

Maureen hesitated for a moment. She couldn't imagine who would have worn that hat last or how she'd look. But what did it matter?

She kept thinking that Amanda would pop out from behind a chair, but she didn't. Raw fear took hold of Maureen. She'd seen on the news and read in newspaper articles about girls being abducted while on vacation, and each time she'd imagined how their parents must have felt. Now she knew. Desperate.

"What if someone calls you while we're gone?" she asked Gordon.

"I have my cell phone." He showed it to her. "All charged."

When they stepped out the front door, Maureen noticed the

162

sky had turned a slate gray. Time had passed. She looped her arm into his to keep her balance. The snow had let up, and her boots slipped on the icy surface. The temperature had plummeted, and the snow had transformed into a sheet of ice. She might as well be ice skating, a skill she'd never mastered.

At that moment, her feet slipped out from under her. She felt Gordon's strong arm keeping her from falling—also her shoulder wrenching out of its socket. But she didn't care about the pain. She was grateful. Never had she felt so powerless on her own.

He opened the passenger door of his Range Rover and helped her climb into it, then closed the door after she was safely inside.

A gentleman, she thought, feeling attracted to him despite her trepidation about Amanda's whereabouts. She knew she needed to focus on her daughter, but she couldn't help glancing at Gordon. Rugged and fearless. And he owned the hotel, for which she was grateful. She and Amanda might move there forever. Well, maybe not forever.

As Maureen let her thoughts drift, she felt the SUV slide to the left. She loved the feel of it until she glanced over and saw Gordon gripping the steering wheel. His face wore a grimace— the corners of his mouth pulled back and his eyes wide open. A moment later the vehicle took a dip and came to a halt in a ditch. She couldn't help herself from gasping as Gordon spewed out what must be Scottish swear words because he glanced to her and said, "*Duilich*—Sorry." He gave her another looking over and asked, "Are you alright?"

Maureen did an internal self-examination. "Yes." But what was he really asking? "Now what?" she said.

"This is but a wee setback. Nothing for you to worry about, lass."

"But my daughter."

"Don't you fret. He hopped out and rounded the rear of the vehicle. He opened the hatchback and pulled out a bag of sand and a shovel.

She should have known he would have thought of everything. "You need help?" she asked, knowing she'd only be in the way.

"No, you sit tight. I'll handle it."

Twenty minutes later, after spinning tires and the vehicle's fishtailing and Gordon digging in the snow, he maneuvered the Land Rover back onto the road. Snow was falling again, blinding Maureen. She feared he'd drive off the road or hit someone.

Through the falling snow, she saw lights. "What's that?"

"Portree." He motored toward the light. "Not much open, except my favorite pub."

Maureen peered out the windshield to see a quaint village cloaked in white.

"The pub's open." Gordon's voice was exuberant. "Let's stop."

"No, I need to find my daughter, not dilly-dally," Maureen said.

"We should stop in ask if anyone has seen her."

"Oh, right. Good idea." Surely someone had. Maureen would die if anything bad happened to Amanda. He pulled up in front of the small establishment, rounded the vehicle, and helped her get out. When he opened the pub's front door, he was met with welcoming voices and a burst of warm air. Gordon seemed to know all of the three dozen or so people perched on stools or crowded into wooden booths.

A large shaggy gray dog lay on the floor near the bar as if a canine in a pub was perfectly normal. Maureen smiled. Denny wasn't the only one in her family to know about dogs.

She spoke to a fellow sitting on a nearby table. "Is that an Irish wolfhound?"

He screwed up his face and pulled his earlobe as if she were speaking gibberish. "No, 'tis a Scottish deerhound."

"Sorry, silly me." Feeling as though she'd put her foot in her mouth, Maureen backed away and moved toward Gordon, but he didn't seem to notice her as he waded deeper and deeper into the crowded pub. The air smelled warm and inviting, enticing Maureen to follow him, not that she had a choice. People, their faces ruddy and gleeful, raised glasses to him and offered to buy him a pint of ale. They spoke with a definite accent, reminding Maureen of the few times Lydia had lapsed into Pennsylvania Dutch. On the other side of the world. Maureen felt off kilter.

The temperature in this place was stifling. Maureen longed to shed her outerwear and ridiculous hat, yet she was also determined to find Amanda. But how? She felt helpless, as if the tide had come in to drown her. But she must not be deterred from her quest. Certainly someone would help her. She dared not call James and admit that she'd lost their daughter. There must be a police station nearby. Although she hadn't seen anyone in uniform.

Gordon finally noticed her and headed her way. "A pint for your lady friend," an older mustached gentleman with a thick Scottish brogue said to Gordon.

"Good idea," Gordon said, nearing the bar and resting his elbow on it. "Me? I'll take a snifter of scotch."

"Coming right up." An array of bottles and a wide mirror spread behind the bartender, a balding man wearing a white apron around his waist. Ignoring the dozens of bottles behind him, he reached under the bar and extracted a bottle and then poured amber-colored liquid into a stout stemmed glass for Gordon. "I hide this scotch from the tourists. I save this for my best customers."

"Hey, I need to find my daughter." Maureen didn't care what they were drinking; she wanted no part of their revelry. She had not come here to party. She wished she'd stayed back at the hotel where she was safe.

A man offered Maureen his stool at the bar. "Have a seat lass."

"No thanks, I won't be staying here long."

The bartender turned to Maureen. "Nothing for me, thanks." She watched the bartender's hands moving—pouring ale and wine, mixing drinks, and passing them to a waitress carrying a tray. "Is there a police station close by?" Maureen asked.

He frowned and shook his head. "Why would you be asking for a policeman when there's brew to be had?"

She caught sight of a young woman sitting at the bar with three men speaking to her. At least someone was enjoying themselves. The woman tittered.

"Amanda?" Maureen recognized her daughter's laughter followed by a man's beefy chuckle. Maureen whipped around to see Amanda sipping a drink two stools away. What on earth? Amanda was drinking red wine?

Maureen garnered the bartender's attention by waving her hands. "Hey, what's the legal age for drinking in Scotland?"

"Eighteen. Unless eating a meal with their parents."

"That young woman is fourteen." Maureen pointed at her daughter, who was wearing enough makeup to hide her age. "Did you ask for her ID?"

"No, because she looked older than that."

Maureen swiveled her head around to evaluate the young woman, but she was gone. Had Maureen imagined seeing her? No, her daughter had no doubt spotted Maureen and then ducked out of sight. Unless another young woman had found the same bottle of redhead color at a drugstore.

Maureen knew it was her own fault for catering to Amanda her whole life, but she feared her daughter had accepted a ride from a stranger. Now what? Maureen imagined all the horrible scenarios. She felt powerless. And angry. Why hadn't Gordon stayed close? She wondered if she could trust him with anything. She recalled when she was in high school. Her parents had been furious when she'd accepted a ride home from a teacher, who had never made one move on her or said anything inappropriate. But now she understood how her parents had felt.

Maureen's gaze canvased the bustling room until they came to rest on Gordon. She leapt off the stool and ran over to him.

"Maureen, my dear," he said, "you look like you've seen a ghost."

She could barely get the words out. "Did you see my daughter?" she asked.

"What does she look like?"

She spoke as loudly as she could to be heard above the din. "Red hair." All conversation around her stopped for a moment, then several people chuckled.

He grinned. "Many a Scottish lass has red hair."

"Bright red. Like a fire engine. If fire engines are even red in Scotland."

The room erupted into laughter and gaiety. Maureen felt herself weaken as the crowd of strangers pressed in. She didn't belong here.

Chapter 43

Lounging in bed, Lydia grasped the handwritten letter from Jonathan. He had sent it to the Cooks' home in New Jersey and it must have been forwarded here. How did he even get the Cooks' address? And did she dare read it? She couldn't bring herself to open the envelope.

She felt like burrowing under the covers and concealing her head for the rest of the day. Because what was she doing here? When given too much freedom she fell into her wicked ways. She needed the parameters of the Amish church. She needed boundaries. Too much freedom was too much temptation for her. If she went home, that horrible man from the shoe store would be waiting for her to take more of her money—or worse.

She would have to confess to her father what she'd done and how she had gotten herself into this jam. Maybe Dat would help her, although she cringed when she thought of the vision of his escorting her to that man's shoe store. She would have to pay the money for the shoes and maybe even confess in front of the whole congregation, which meant embarrassing her parents. But she had to own up to the truth. She was a shoplifter—a petty thief. She would have been better off in jail, now that she thought about it. Better off being arrested than being caught in the snare of deception. She couldn't run away from the truth.

Jonathan's face—first as the lad she'd grown up with, then his handsome features, his steely blue eyes—crystalized in her mind, making her long for him. And the smoky depth of his voice as he had matured over the years. She relived his last kiss. Maybe their final embrace. Did he even care for her anymore? Maybe he had written her to tell heard that he'd found someone better. Would he care for her once he learned of her dishonesty?

She tore open the envelope, pulled out the handwritten letter, and whispered aloud: "Dear Lydia, this is the last time I will try to reach you. I give up. I don't know what I've done that is wrong, but I must assume you no longer wish to have me court you. My parents and friends tell me to find someone new, and they have a woman in mind. Is that what you want? My parents are encouraging me to meet a new woman in the district who recently moved here from Kentucky with three young children."

Ach, he was jumping to all the wrong conclusions. Or was he? Lydia had some soul searching to do, as the Englischers would say. Life was so much simpler when her decisions were made for her. She saw now that they were in her best interest.

She forced herself to get up and leave the room. Entering the hallway, she took a left and rapped on Maureen and Amanda's door, but all was silent. As Lydia pivoted to descend the stairs, she expected to see or hear Amanda and Maureen, but the dining room lay empty and quiet. She was surprised to see dirty plates in need of clearing on the tables. And soiled napkins laying helter-skelter.

She followed her nose to the kitchen where she heard subdued voices and came upon Denny and Alec, their heads tilted together and their voices subdued. Denny seemed to be crying. Crying over what? Then all fell silent.

Denny and Alec parted, but their eyes locked on each other. It seemed as though they were going to kiss, but then Denny noticed Lydia.

Denny's face turned angry. "Where is Amanda?" she asked. "You scared my sister half to death." Denny peered behind Lydia, who winced.

"Ach, I thought she was with you."

Denny looked around the kitchen. "Well, as you can see, she isn't." Denny had a way of making Lydia feel inadequate, but she

169

knew in truth that she had no reason to expect more. Lydia was hired help not a family member or a friend brought along on a carefree vacation to have fun. She had a job, but she had taken advantage of the situation. For all she knew, Maureen would fire her.

"She must be around here somewhere," Lydia said, scoping the kitchen and seeing Molly and a young man filling the dishwasher. Ach, Lydia had promised to help tidy the dining room and kitchen. She grabbed an apron off a hook and tied it on. "I'm so sorry."

"Never mind the kitchen when Amanda is missing," Denny said.

Lydia felt foolish asking, "Where's Maureen?"

"Darned if I know," Denny said. "She took off with Gordon somewhere."

"Have you tried contacting her?" Lydia asked.

"Knowing my sister, her cell phone is sitting by her bed upstairs."

"I have Gordon's number," Alec said. "I'll give him a jingle."

"That would be wonderful." Denny said. "Now if we could only get the veterinarian here."

"What for?" Lydia asked.

"It's Princess. She's sick."

"Let me run down and check on her," Lydia said.

"What for?" Denny's voice was tight and angry. "We need a veterinarian, but she said she can't make it through the storm. If Princess dies, how will we care for her puppies?"

Lydia spun toward the stairs to the basement and trotted down the steps until she reached Princess, who stood panting in labored breaths. She growled at Lydia, but Lydia would not be deterred if there was any way she could help this poor animal and her litter. Lydia thought of the many times she had assisted her father out in the barn. Cows with their bawling calves, sheep with their newborn lambs, mares tending their foals. She was grateful for Dat's calling on her for assistance. He had taught her much. Lydia moved next to Princess and felt her teats. Just as she thought. Mastitis, an engorged breast—hard and warm. A death sentence if ignored.

Princess looked up at her as if imploring help.

Lydia scrambled up the stairs. "Quick, I need warm water and towels." She turned her attention to Molly and said, "Cabbage leaves would be best if you have them."

"Okay." While Denny put hot water on the stove, Lydia rifled through the vegetable compartment until she found green cabbage. "These will work fine." Lydia tore off a dozen outer leaves. "Don't let that water get up to boiling." She turned down the heat and dipped the cabbage leaves in. Then she carried the pan down to the basement with care and started working on Princess's hardened teat, warming and then massaging it until milk showed itself. Just a spot of milk but a good sign. She knew Princess was grateful, even if she couldn't say so. Princess settled down and lay in her bed.

"You can bring the puppies back," Lydia told Denny.

"Princess won't need to go to the vet?" Denny asked.

"No, I think we averted the catastrophe." Lydia attempted to keep the pride out of her voice. She assisted in returning the puppies to Princess, who relaxed and lay on her side so the pups could nurse.

At least Lydia had done one thing right for which she was grateful. But where was Amanda?

Chapter 44

Denny was blown away by Lydia's skill in caring for Princess. Only an hour ago Princess had seemed one step away from death, but now the mama dog was licking and cleaning her pups. And they were suckling with gusto. Denny was pleased to see Rosie getting plenty of attention from Princess. Denny admonished herself for not offering Princess water sooner. Denny had been paralyzed by fear. In some ways, she was a dummy, and Lydia had the smarts. Maybe in most ways.

Denny felt Alec's presence behind her. She wondered if he was mesmerized by Princess and the puppies or by Lydia. No use sulking, Denny told herself. An unattractive trait that was sure to scare Alec away. So she decided to do something drastically different from her ordinary self.

"You were amazing, Lydia." Lydia's face showed surprise. "Thank you so much for saving Princess and the pups. Especially Rosie, who is nearest and dearest to my heart."

"It was nothing," Lydia said. "Mastitis is common on the farm, and veterinarians are far and few between. Not that we don't hire them when needed."

"You should think about becoming a veterinarian," Alec said. "You're so good with animals."

"That would mean going to veterinarian school. I would never be accepted. I've only graduated from eighth grade."

Denny couldn't contain a sputter of laughter. "You're kidding." But Lydia didn't answer.

Alec neared her. "Did I hear you right?" he asked Lydia. "But why?"

"The Ordnung, our set of rules we Amish must live by. Amish children attend school only through eighth grade, then they focus on learning a trade." Lydia shrugged. "As you can see, I am not following the Ordnung." She patted her hair. "Ach, why did I cut my hair? I could kill myself."

"That seems a bit drastic. It will grow back." Denny tried to console Lydia, when in fact she had no idea what Lydia was talking about. Why shouldn't she style her hair the way she wanted?

"It will eventually grow back but not for years and years," Lydia said. "I can't believe I cut off my hair. Surely, I will burn in hell and deserve to."

"As I said, it will grow back," Denny said. "Cutting your hair can't be the worst thing you've ever done."

"That's the truth." But Lydia didn't elaborate. Denny was dying to know more but didn't ask. Not with Alec here.

Denny scooted around her to pet Rosie. She wondered why she was drawn so much to this one pup but decided to accept the fact that she was. Like love at first sight. And Princess seemed to like Denny and accept the fact that she was a city girl and helpless when Princess had needed drastic intervention. For a moment, Denny considered attending veterinary school herself. What was stopping her, other than laziness? And money. And good health. She'd accumulated decent grades in college when she'd studied English literature. But would a veterinary college consider that worth a hoot? In hindsight she wished she had studied science. Particularly biology. But none of this mattered if she had cancer eating away at her like a savage pack of hungry wolves. She never should have come on this trip. Not true. Because she wouldn't have met Alec and found her darling Rosie. But would Gordon sell her? She envisioned herself going home alone to her apartment and her empty bookstore. Part of the reason she'd come on this trip was to buy books. But there was no way she could buy them in this storm. She glanced to the window and saw white.

"What are you thinking about," Alec asked her.

"My mind was wandering." Humongous lies, insignificant lies. Denny's life was a mountain of duplicity. Maybe everyone's life was built upon falsehoods. Was there an honest person left on this earth? Should she admit to him that she was possibly dying? She bet that Lydia was honest. Of all the people she knew, Lydia seemed the most honest. Which made Denny dislike her all the more. There, she'd been honest with herself. Honest enough to admit that she despised Lydia. Little Miss Perfect. And yet she hadn't kept an eye on Amanda. Where was the girl?

Denny couldn't breathe. She imagined herself in Maureen's shoes and felt panic encompass her. Maureen must be scared to death. If only their father was still alive. He would swoop in and save the day. He had been a take-charge type of man, who had all the answers. Their mother too. She stayed calm during a crisis. But both of their parents were dead. No nice way to put it. Denny found the term *passed* disgusting. They hadn't passed. They'd expired. Denny's throat tightened, and her lungs wouldn't expand.

"I just called Gordon," Alec said, breaking through Denny's bonds of anxiety. "I could barely hear him above the noise of the pub."

"They're in a pub this time of day?" Outrage inundated Denny at the thought of Maureen and Gordon in a warm pub, drinking and whooping it up. "Have they found Amanda?"

"Doesn't sound like it. Has she done this kind of thing before?"

Denny heard a vehicle, chains on its tires, in the distance. "Not that I know of." Denny turned her head toward Alec. "She is a bit of a prankster." Denny was making light of a serious situation because in fact she had never known Amanda to run away from home. Where could she go, and how would she get there?

174

Chapter 45

Maureen set about asking everyone in the small, bustling pub if they had seen a redheaded fourteen-year-old, but each shook their head. She felt herself crumbling. A few smirked, leaving Maureen in dismay and about to have a meltdown. "I'm her mother," she finally yelled, followed by chortling.

"And I'm her father."

"What?" Maureen spun around. "James?" she said to her husband. Was she hallucinating?

He looked down his aristocratic nose at her. "You have more than one husband?"

"No. But how did you get here?"

"I hired a private jet after Amanda texted me and told me you were leaving me for another man." He looked the room over. "I'd like to meet this bozo."

"He's not a bozo, and I don't know where she got the idea that I was leaving you."

"Amanda isn't always straight with me, but I truly doubt she'd make up a story like that. She begged me to come. Where is she?"

"I have no idea."

None of his story rang true. How and why would James come here?

"Where is that little smarty pants?" His gaze scanned the crowded pub.

Maureen felt too depleted to give him a full explanation. "How did you get here?" She felt as if she'd been sucked into a zany dream from which she couldn't escape.

He flapped his arms. "I just told you. In a private jet. And then I hired a four-wheel-drive Uber with chains." He tapped his forehead in a condescending manner. "Remember I was a Boy Scout. Be prepared."

"But I don't understand how you knew where to come."

"I tracked you on your Apple AirTag. Out of sight but never out of mind."

"You stalked me?" Maureen felt flooded with anger—and yet flattered that he'd gone to so much trouble to track her down.

"Only for your own safety." His smirking face grinned down at her. "If you lost your purse or luggage—that sort of thing. Say, I stopped by the hotel just now and spoke to your sister." He had never liked Denny and vice versa. Maureen could not imagine Denny's giving him a cordial welcome.

James widened his stance. "She confirmed that you have a love interest."

"She did?"

"Yeah, and I'd like to meet him—if you don't mind."

Gordon stepped up beside him. Gordon stood a full six inches taller, so James could not look down his nose at him.

When James noticed him, he moved away so that he could scrutinize Gordon's face. Maureen assessed bearded Gordon. Not that she considered him her lover. But if she stayed here long enough, who knows what might happen?

Maureen lifted her chin. "Right now, my first priority is finding Amanda."

"I can't believe you let her slip through your fingers." James's voice rose in pitch and volume. "What kind of a mother are you?"

"From what I've seen she's a wonderful mother." Gordon moved into the conversation. "She got me to drive out in the storm looking for Amanda."

James whirled around to speak to Gordon. "Listen, buddy, shove off."

"You want a fight?" Gordon grabbed hold of James's collar.

Maureen could envision them groveling on the floor. Gordon would be the victor, for sure.

The bustling room fell silent. A long moment ensued. Maureen had seen her husband lose his temper many times and feared the worst.

"Daddy, Daddy, you came." Amanda ran over and hugged James around the waist. "I can't believe you came all this way."

"Of course, I did." James wrapped an arm around her. He draped his other arm around Maureen's shoulder, a rare occurrence. "There isn't anything I wouldn't do for my two favorite girls."

Empty man-talk, Maureen thought. Nothing more.

Gordon did not shrink back. If anything, he stood taller. My, oh my, what a handsome brute of a fellow. But Maureen was not about to divorce her husband on a whim. Yet, how could she continue to remain married to a man who treated her like chattel? A mere possession.

Maureen knew she should punish Amanda—James obviously wasn't going to—but she was beyond thankful her daughter was safe. Yet her head was inundated with questions.

"How did you get here from the hotel?" She spoke to Amanda using her sternest voice.

"I hitchhiked." Amanda put out her thumb and wiggled her hips. "Easy-peasy. A guy in a truck with four-wheel drive stopped and gave me a ride."

"A stranger?" Maureen was horrified as she replayed all the nightmarish possible scenarios.

"Chill out," Amanda said. "By the time we got here, he wasn't a stranger anymore."

"This is how you take care of our daughter?" James's face turned red with rage.

"Hold on," Gordon said. "This is one of the safest places on earth."

James swung around to face him. "Says the man who is trying the steal my wife?"

"I never would steal another man's wife." Gordon folded his

beefy arms across his chest. "Even though she be a Campbell. Or so I've been told."

The crowd around them hushed and drew closer.

"Well, is she a Campbell?" Gordon asked.

"So what if she is?" James's eyes zeroed in on Gordon's. Then in a moment of fury, his fist balled and jutted out to sock Gordon's jaw. Gordon fell backward on the floor.

"How dare you?" Gordon soothed his face for a moment, then sprang to his feet and came at James, pushing him.

The two men grappled, tipped over chairs. Cheering and placing bets, the crowd egged them on.

"Stop," Maureen yelled, but her voice was lost amidst the crashing of breaking wood, laughter, and shouting.

Maureen was fascinated to see her husband and Gordon fighting over her—if that's what they were doing. She would never understand men.

Amanda came streaking over to them and said, "Get off my dad," her voice barely audible over the cheering of the pub patrons. In her hand, she supported a meat pie, which she hurled at Gordon but missed him. Hit a bearded man in the face.

The man swiped his face. "How dare you—"

A moment later, a woman, who might have been his wife or girlfriend, threw her sandwich at Amanda.

James clambered to his feet. Looking disheveled, he was panting. "Leave—my daughter alone."

"That little brat is your daughter?" Gordon got to his feet. "Makes sense."

The proprietor ran over to them. "Have you gone daft? No food fight or I'll kick you all out in the snow."

Maureen scanned the crowded pub. As if frozen in time, they all were looking at James and Gordon. She guessed they were hoping for a spectacle—a brawl.

James broke the ice when he said, "Drinks for everyone in the house on me." A loud cheer with hoots resounded, filling the room.

Chapter 46

Lydia wished she had gone with Maureen. Now what would she do with herself for the rest of the day? For the rest of her life would be a better way of putting it because after today she might not have a job. Sure, Maureen treated her well enough, but this might be the last straw, as Dat would say.

She noticed Mrs. Ross dusting. Lydia gathered her courage to speak to her. She couldn't imagine what the older woman thought of her after she'd broken all that china but what did she have to lose? "I wonder if you need to hire new employees after this terrible snow," Lydia said.

Mrs. Ross tilted her head. "What would the snow have to do with anything? We'll not be firing anyone that we told could take the time off."

Lydia felt her cheeks warming. "Of course you wouldn't, but will you hire more people during the warmer months when you have more business?"

"You are speaking to the wrong person. The hotel's owner, Gordon McDonald, makes all those decisions, not I." She continued her dusting. "I suppose you could help me right now. I need someone to set the tables. Not that we have many people staying at the hotel." She turned to face Lydia. "Be sure not to break anything."

"Yes, madam." Lydia's first urge was to defend herself but no matter. "I'd be glad to help in any way I can. Just tell me what to do." She refolded a napkin. "And I'll be extra careful."

Mrs. Ross looked out the window. "I can't believe the snow is

179

still falling. I doubt any customers will come in today. Or any staff for that matter. Several have called, and I told them to stay home."

It occurred to Lydia that this was the perfect time to prove herself. She would show Mrs. Ross what a competent worker she was.

Lydia straightened a table setting. No use putting more flatware out until customers actually came in. "I'm at your command until Maureen gets back. Please ask me to do anything."

Mrs. Ross assessed Lydia's outfit. "If you are going to be out here with our customers, then I'd like you to wear a kilt. Would you have a problem with that?"

"Not in the slightest. In fact, I'd love it."

"We have some extras in the storage room."

Lydia was tickled with the idea.

"All right then," Mrs. Ross said. "In the meantime, check on the coffee urn and water in the kettle in the kitchen. I'll be right back."

"Yes, I will." Lydia was filled with hope and delight as she dashed into the kitchen and did as she was told.

Minutes later Mrs. Ross brought Lydia a plaid kilt. "This kilt might be a bit large for such a wee slip of a thing. As you can see, it can be cinched to fit your slim waist." She held it up. "But there's nothing to be done about that length."

"I don't mind. I'm used to wearing long skirts."

Mrs. Ross cast her a look of doubt. "If you say so." Mrs. Ross unfolded the kilt and held it up to Lydia. "This seems to be the shortest one, and yet it's too long for you."

Lydia took the kilt from her. "I can make it work." She wrapped it around her slender frame, and it cascaded to the floor. But not too long.

"Have you ever worked in a restaurant before?"

"Yes—I mean no." Lydia was determined to tell the truth. "But I come from a large family, and I'm used to waiting on people." She scooped up a couple of menus. "I'm sure I can manage."

"Until the owner gets back that's fine. He is the one who will make the decision. And don't you work for Maureen Cook?"

"Under the circumstances, I think she'll want me to help you." Lydia adored the feel of the wool fabric on her legs. She wondered if she could sew such a complicated garment—how the red, green, and blue plaid were folded and sewn around her hips was still a mystery—the opposite of what she was used to. At her waist, two buckles secured it. She'd never fastened buckles at her waist. Too fancy. She shuddered to imagine what her father's reaction would be.

"Here's a vest." Mrs. Ross handed Lydia a lovely olive-green vest with matching buttons down the front.

Lydia ran her hands across the velveteen's smooth surface. "Thank you so much."

"It is you who is helping us." Mrs. Ross sent her a smile—maybe the first genuine show of kindness since Lydia had arrived. But then she remembered the broken china in the kitchen.

"I can help pay off the cost of the china today if that's all right with you."

"That's a wonderful idea." Mrs. Ross's expression turned serious—her mouth pursed. "But please try not to break anything else."

"I'll be ever so careful."

"The newlyweds might have placed an order outside their door. How would you feel about preparing it and bringing it up to them?"

"I'll go check and get working on it right away," Lydia said.

Mrs. Ross handed her a slip of paper. "Last night they ordered enough to feed an army, but it's what they ordered, so Molly brought it to them." She glanced down at the paper, then back up to Lydia's eyes as if assessing her ability. "Have you ever made hollandaise sauce before? And what about poached eggs?"

"I'm sure I can manage. If nothing else, I can look in a cookbook."

"Here, try this one." Mrs. Ross handed her a dogeared hardcover book.

Lydia cracked the book and checked in the back for a

hollandaise sauce recipe. Her mouth watered as she scanned the ingredients. In her mind she could taste the melted butter whisked together with egg yolks and lemon juice. "Yah, I can make this if you find me the Dijon mustard." She didn't think Mam kept it in her pantry. She reread the recipe and her vision landed on *cayenne pepper*. The recipe called for only a pinch so it must be strong or zesty. She'd never heard of it but didn't dare ask Mrs. Ross. If only Mam was here to help her.

"We serve nothing but the very best," Mrs. Ross said. "And it must be garnished. Do you know what I'm talking about?"

Lydia wasn't sure she did, but she nodded. Ach, she had lied again. "I'll do my very best." That was the truth. She would if it killed her.

"Since we're low on staff, I will rely on you to work the cash register too." Mrs. Ross moved toward a modern cash register, pushed a button, and opened it. "What have we here? It's empty, save for a few coins." She swung around to Lydia and said, "Did you open this and remove cash?"

"No, as God is my witness, I did not take anything." Lydia knew that invoking the Lord's name was against the teaching of the Ordnung, but too late to take the words back now.

Ach, no matter her clothes, nor hair—try as she might—she wasn't Englisch. And never would be. She felt as if she were floating in the middle of nowhere. She didn't belong here nor did she belong back in New Jersey living with Maureen and James in their plush house watching TV and using electrical appliances. Or scrolling through the internet for hours as she waited for Amanda to get home from school, then cajoled the stubborn girl to do her homework.

But Lydia intended on following through the best she could. She hustled up the stairs to the newlyweds' room and found that they had written their lunchorder and placed it outside their door atop a mountain of dirty dishes. Lydia wouldn't mind getting a look at them but figured they wanted privacy, which is what she would want on her honeymoon should she ever go on one. Should she ever get married.

Back in the kitchen, she located an oval silver tray with a handle at each end. She polished its tarnished surface until it shone. Then she placed two folded cloth napkins and flatware with care upon it. She took a moment to admire her creation and hoped the newlyweds would approve. Not to mention Mrs. Ross.

"I've thought of a job for you while we wait for the food orders to come in." Mrs. Ross seemed pleased with herself. "How are you at making beds?"

"I can do that for you." Lydia suddenly felt confident. "Just tell me what you need, and I'll gladly do it."

Mrs. Ross gathered several room keys and held them out. "All these rooms still have dirty sheets on the beds, and they need cleaning, now that I think about it. Could you manage that?"

"Yah. Do you have a washer and dryer?" Lydia was glad she'd used Maureen's so many times. Her mam had taught her to make beds neatly and she'. In truth Lydia was proud of her housekeeping abilities, but she mustn't puff up like a rooster.

"Well then, I can keep you busy for as long as it takes Mrs. Cook to return. Which may be a while." Mrs. Ross glanced out the window. "It doesn't look as if the snow is letting up."

Chapter 47

Denny felt a fire kindling inside her chest each time she came in close proximity to Alec. She reminded herself not to do anything stupid such as take his hand, which she longed to do. Or snuggle into him. She imagined his strong arms wrapping around her, keeping her safe.

But he might rebuke her. He might be repulsed for all she knew. What did she know about Scottish men, and whom could she ask? Not Mrs. Ross, who was too old.

"Is Molly still in the hotel?" she asked Alec.

"No idea. I haven't seen her lately." He glanced into the dining room. "It looks as though Mrs. Ross has put Lydia to work."

Denny tried not to gawk at graceful Lydia clad in a kilt. "I'd love to wear a kilt like that," Denny said as if she'd been pondering the idea for days. "What fun. Are there extras?"

"I think so, but you'd have to ask Mrs. Ross." The corners of his mouth tipped up into a smile. "She tried to get me to wear one, but I refused." His eyebrows lifted. "Not that I don't hang onto my childhood kilt."

"You'd look cute." Denny thought he'd look cute anytime but decided to say no more. Her mother whispered from beyond the grave for Denny to act with discretion.

"When the snow lets up, you can have one made for you in Portree."

"Really? I'd love that." Denny couldn't contain her goofy grin.

"But I can't imagine any of the stores carry your tartan." He shrugged. "Maybe things have changed."

"We have a saying where I come from: old habits die hard." When she noticed his look of confusion, she added, "But I'm not sure it fits in this case."

"Alas, it fits all too well."

"But you don't hate me, do you? Please tell me you forgive my ancestors for their ghastly behavior."

He cast her a sideways look, his eyes not meeting hers. "Aye, our generation has forgiven. But my parents… some of them cling to the past and hold grudges."

"You want to introduce me to your parents?" How cool was that? But would they like her?

Like a cloud across the sun, his features sobered. "Hold on, lassie. Let's not rush into anything."

"No, of course not. We hardly know each other." Denny had put the cart before the horse, as they say, as she'd often done in the past. "Why would they wish to meet me?"

"I might have mentioned you on a phone call."

"You mentioned me to your folks?" As Denny waited for an answer, she pressed her lips together while her thoughts raced like a horse out of the gate at the Kentucky Derby—which she loved watching on TV. "Say, what about Molly? I couldn't help but notice you two have a certain closeness."

"Yes we do, for sure, but they're not expecting me to marry Molly of all people."

"They aren't?" Denny had suspected something lovey-dovey between Alec and Molly all along. No big deal. Wrong. It was a big deal. Ginormous.

Denny recalled the night her date had not showed up for the senior prom, something she thought she'd pushed out of her memory forever. She recalled mustering up the courage to invite Steve from the popular crowd. "I guess so" was his answer, and she'd given him her home address. He'd crammed the paper into his jeans pocket. She remembered getting all spruced up in a dress her mother had helped her buy and going with Mom to the salon to get a manicure. Mom had helped her with her hair and applying makeup. "You look stunning," her mother had said when Denny examined herself in the mirror.

Denny had waited by the front door, but her date never arrived. Nor did he call. No explanation. She'd convinced herself he'd had car trouble. She'd called her girlfriend who was waiting for her steady date to arrive. "Come with us," her friend had urged. "Lots of girls go by themselves." But Denny felt too shameful. Once her tears erupted, her eye makeup melted, making her look like an owl.

She thought she had pushed that wretched night behind her but realized she'd carried it with her all this time. She recalled with clarity how the next week she'd begged her mother to let her stay home sick from school, but Mom had refused. "I'm so sorry, but you'll have to go back sometime darling. Try to ignore him."

Easier said than done.

At school Denny had lifted her chin as if the incident never happened. But her no-show date and his friends had snickered at her as she passed them in the hallways. Yet she was determined not to show any hurt. She'd sworn she would never make such a fool of herself again. But wasn't that exactly what she was doing with Alec? What was his game? He said he'd mentioned her to his parents but he seemed to be attracted to Molly. Since the death of her parents, she didn't think anything could hurt her, but she felt as if she'd been stabbed by a kitchen knife.

Alec's words jolted her to the present. "Do you want to try to make it to Portree today?" he asked. "It's not a long walk."

"No thanks. Maybe when Maureen returns." Denny heard her voice turn snarly. "She's the one who is paying you."

He visibly deflated, his shoulders rounding and his smile flattening.

"And I wouldn't want to take you away from Molly." She tried to act nonchalantly. "By the way, when's the wedding?" When he didn't answer, she added, "I do hope I'll be invited."

Chapter 48

Maureen was appalled as she scanned the small pub. Where once harmony reigned, chaos prevailed. Chairs lay tipped on their sides, chards of broken glass sparkled across the wooden floor, and the volume in the room, albeit filled with laughter and good humor, was so loud that Maureen felt like plugging her ears.

All because of James's arrival. He'd hurled the first verbal dart and the first fist at Gordon's jaw. She had to admit she admired his proficiency. She had no idea her husband was capable of a right hook. But Maureen reminded herself she had never cared for violence of any kind. All along, Amanda had clapped her hands and jumped up and down. "Punch him, Daddy, punch him." Where had Amanda picked up such uncouth manners? Most girls would be embarrassed.

Several patrons helped gather up broken furniture and set it aside, as if it was no big deal. "And I'll pay for any damage." Gordon said to the bartender. "A pint of ale for me. And buy this gentleman the best scotch in the house, no matter the cost."

When James heard this, he seemed to settle down and lose all animosity. "That's awfully good of you," he said to Gordon, as if they were old chums. The two men shook hands, much to Maureen's astonishment.

But where was Amanda? Maureen took James's elbow and asked him the same question. "What happened to Amanda? She was here just a moment ago."

James pulled away from her grasp. "How would I know? You're the one who brought her here."

"Is she not your daughter too?" Sometimes Maureen hated James and his glib answers. He could answer any question with another question, which must come in handy in the courtroom. But she was tired of living in a verbal tug-of-war, where she always lost. If she pulled too hard and he let go, she would fall on her rear end. Hang on or let go, he always won.

"We're talking about our daughter," she said. "And she told me she's pregnant." Amanda had recanted her provocative statement, but why let James know? Maureen decided it was his turn to suffer.

"She'd better not be."

"Or what?" Maureen asked. "You'll disown her?"

Chapter 49

Lydia's hand shook as she extracted her cell phone and tapped in Jonathan's number. Neither one of them was supposed to own a cell phone, but they did, against the teachings of the Ordnung. She reminded herself that neither one of them had been baptized into the Amish faith, which helped, but still what she was doing was wrong. She wondered how Jonathan would react. Her best guess was that he would tell her he was courting someone else and no longer cared for Lydia. Which she deserved. She hadn't contacted him for months. Not even a letter or a postcard as she had promised to do. No answer, so she left a message. She tried to keep her voice upbeat but imagined it through his ears. As she spoke, she considered the fact that he might be ignoring her phone call. Would she blame him? But something in her prodded her on.

"Hello, Jonathan. It's L-Lydia… calling to say hi. And to apologize for being so rude. I should have called or written to you months ago like I promised. I kept waiting for the perfect moment." She was lying, and she knew it. "I'm still working for Maureen Cook, taking care of her daughter. Although this might be hard to believe, we are in Scotland on an island called Skye. On the other side of the Atlantic Ocean." Ach, she wished she had rehearsed her conversation better. "If you can find it in your heart to speak to me, please call so I can fill you in. This trip has gone awry to put it mildly."

As she stashed her phone, she listened to the silence. She glanced down at her kilt and enjoyed the way it swished at the bottom. Jonathan would not approve, nor would he approve of her hair bobbed short. He would be repulsed no doubt. She considered whether she could hide her hair beneath a heart-shaped cap until they got married. She knew her hair would take years and years to grow back. But she would be forgiven if she repented. One of her friend's oldest brothers had jumped the fence—left the Amish community and lived as Englischers. Even though they were not allowed to eat at the table with the family, they could dine at a separate table. Their mam had begged them to return to no avail.

She raked her fingers through her hair. Why on earth had she decided to cut it to begin with? But then why had she done so many outlandish things? Always, she had longed for more than the plain life. Enough to steal for it. And be blackmailed. If she went back to Lancaster County, she would confess all her transgressions and be humiliated. Which she deserved to be. Yes. Maybe a kneeling confession before the whole congregation would set her free.

"Here you go." Mrs. Ross handed her a stack of clean linens, rousing her out of her ruminations. "Tear down the beds and remake them, if you're still willing."

"Yah, I am. Happy to." Enjoying the swish of the kilt against her legs, Lydia followed Mrs. Ross up the staircase. She knocked on a door, waited a moment, then opened it.

"What a mess." Mrs. Ross harrumphed. "But I suppose they left in a hurry when the electricity went out and will want their money back."

"I can take care of it." Lydia would never leave a room in such disarray—the covers and sheets and pillows on the floor. But she was determined to prove to Mrs. Ross that she could take care of anything. As she pulled the sheets off and tossed them by the door, she noticed something on the bed stand. A string of pearls grabbed her attention. She was tempted to take them and hide them in her pocket. She prayed for strength but found none. She took hold of them and felt marvelous cool smoothness like marbles in her hand. But where would she put them? As far as she could tell, this kilt did not have pockets, and the vest had but one small pocket not big enough to hide a string of pearls.

She imagined the scene that would follow if she stole them. Whoever had rented this room would surely call and ask about them. Mrs. Ross might summon the police and have her arrested, which is exactly what she deserved if she took them. Maureen might fire her. Well, of course she would. Lydia would be sent home in disgrace.

Ignoring the pearls, Lydia vacuumed and dusted, then made the bed using neat precise motions to make it as perfect as possible—the way Mam had taught her. Finally, Lydia pulled up the quilt and arranged the pillows. A moment later Mrs. Ross surprised her by opening the door. "That looks beautiful," the older woman said.

"I found something." Lydia pointed to the bed table. "In their hurry, someone left a string of pearls."

"Oh, my, I'm lucky to have an honest girl like you helping me." Mrs. Ross moved over to her and scooped them up. "Thank you."

When was the last time someone had called Lydia honest? She was filled with a warmth of pride—not the bad kind of pride that her dat warned her against. Self-respect is what she felt. Now if she could just continue to conduct herself in such a way.

Mrs. Ross led her to several other rooms. With speed and agility, Lydia vacuumed the carpets, dusted the furniture, made the beds, and straightened the areas. It occurred to Lydia that she had learned her most useful abilities at home under the watchful eye of her parents. Not that she could vacuum at home without electricity. In truth, the vacuum was too loud for her ears. She would just as soon sweep and mop the floor.

The Englisch life held too many temptations, and she had already proved to herself that she could not resist them. She was determined to overcome her weaknesses. Starting now.

Chapter 50

When Denny saw Alec and Molly hugging each other she felt as if she'd walked into a glass window. She gasped. She couldn't stop herself.

Noticing her, the couple stepped apart. But Denny knew what she'd seen. They were hiding something from her. Or trying to. But what?

"Hello." Alec smiled. A phony smile as far as Denny could see. Well, he was a phony, just like her last boyfriend. Leave it to her to set her sights on another phony. Which made Denny feel ashamed of herself for being taken in. Again.

Denny stood there gawking at them. "Well?" she finally said. "Will one of you tell me what's going on."

"In a couple of months, we're moving to America." Molly's buoyant voice revealed excitement and happiness.

"Not as a couple," Alec said. "As good friends."

Did they expect Denny to believe them? She felt like laughing, but instead tears pressed at the back of her eyes.

"I hope you're both very happy together." Denny forced her words out but could not form her mouth into a genuine smile.

"We'll be living in Connecticut with my sister and her husband." Molly glanced to Alec. "They have an updated barn with bedrooms and a bathroom," she said.

"That's wonderful." Denny reminded herself she didn't need a man. Men were nothing but pond scum if the past was the best predictor of the future.

Denny decided to make a speedy exit, but as she turned to

leave so did Alec. He stepped aside to let her pass. More proof that he couldn't wait to be rid of her. She felt like kicking him in the shins. Not that it would help her cause in any way.

He took her upper arm. "What's your hurry?" he asked.

Was this guy for real? "Let go of me." She wrestled out of his grasp.

He released her arm. "Sorry, lassie." He seemed to be staring at a speck on her shoulder. "No offense meant."

Denny felt mortified and stupid. She looked into Alec's handsome face and saw round eyes and a gaping jaw. Clearly, she had misjudged his innocent action.

"No, I'm the one who's sorry," Denny said.

"Something going on I should know about?" Molly's hands clasped her hips.

Alec looked from woman to woman. "I'm afraid Denny's got the wrong idea about us."

"As would anyone, my wee man," Molly said.

Alec narrowed his eyes at her. "I'm not your wee little anything. And I'll thank you not to call me that. Ever again."

"Since when did you get to be so uppity?" Molly's dimples deepened. "A fine couple we'd make."

Alec rotated toward Denny. "It's not what you think."

Denny bristled. "And how would you know what I think?" Denny used her sternest voice. "I don't appreciate being caught in the middle of a lovers' spat."

Molly burst into a peel of laughter. Which stoked Denny into wrath. As far as she could see, both Molly and Alec were ridiculing her. Well, what did she care? All she wanted was to bring her darling puppy, Rosie, home with her to her bookshop. To build a thriving business. Was that out of the question without her father's financial support and business savvy? She needed to get her priorities in order—that was one thing for sure.

Maybe Alec and Molly would help her if she played her cards right, as they say. She tried to convince herself they were suited for each other. Maybe Denny would die an old maid, but so be it. She wouldn't be alone if she had Rosie to keep her company. She needed to get things squared away with Gordon. But how?

"Any news about Amanda?" she asked without actually looking into Alec's or Molly's eyes.

They both answered, "No," simultaneously, proving to Denny what she already knew. They were a couple, joined at the hip, soon to move to America to be wed. Denny let out a deep sigh and admonished herself for being so silly. She tried to remember if any man had ever loved her and couldn't come up with a single name. Not down-to-the-bone love.

She gathered herself up and stood tall. No more victim mentality. She wandered into the dining room and saw it as the perfect place for a wedding. Maybe Alec and Molly would get married before moving to America.

She imagined a huge wedding cake decorated just the way she'd wanted. Buttery icing and white flowers to match her wedding dress. She knew it was ridiculous for her to be daydreaming of her own wedding. I mean, who was the groom and who would give her away? But she allowed her musings to meander. Maureen could be her matron of honor, and Amanda could be her flower girl. She smiled at the thought of it, then recalled Amanda was still missing. Who knew what kind of trouble the girl could get herself into if left on her own? But for all Denny knew, Amanda had hitchhiked into town and had been invited into a Scottish home with other teenagers for a meal. She was enjoying chatting with her new friends. Denny wished she'd had such moxie at that age instead of caring so much about what all the other kids thought about her. If honest with herself, she still did care. Too much.

"Have you two decided to wait to get married until you get to the United States?" she asked them. "This room would be a perfect venue for a wedding."

Molly scanned the dining room. "Aren't you sweet?" She sidled up next to Denny. "If we did, would you wish to be one of my bridesmaids?"

"I could. But I didn't bring clothing that would match the other women's dresses."

"No matter. As long as you enjoy music and can dance the Highland fling."

"What?" Denny had at a young age attended a local Highland Games with the family. Her father had insisted they go as a family even though Denny complained because she wanted to hang out with a friend who had a swimming pool in her back yard. But once at the Highland Games, much to Denny's surprise, she'd thoroughly enjoyed herself.

"Alec and I have won competitions dancing together." Molly stood on one leg and raised her other and bent it at the knee. Then she pointed to her foot on her raised leg to demonstrate her superb balance and grace.

"I can't dance worth a hoot." Denny felt clumsy even speaking about her awkwardness. "I have two left feet."

"You at least like bagpipes, don't you?" Molly moved closer. "And the fiddle and the stock-and-horn."

"I love the bagpipe. But I've never heard of that last one."

"But surely you know what an accordion is and a tin whistle, and a cittern—it's like a small guitar, only better because it makes one want to dance. You won't be able to stop yourself."

Denny did not appreciate being put on the spot but kept a smile upon her face. "I like bagpipes best." Denny felt a yearning every time she heard the moaning of a distant bagpipe.

But dance to one at Molly and Alec's wedding with a fake grin plastered on her face? That was a different matter.

"Let's put this foolishness to sleep." Alec turned his full attention to Denny. "Molly's pulling your leg. We don't plan to be wed. Ever." As he peered into her eyes, Denny felt herself melt. "How can I redeem myself?" he asked.

"Are ya daft?" Molly stepped closer. "Get her Rosie— whatever it takes. She loves that little pup more than she loves you."

"But Gordon is a man not easily swayed."

"How about a nice game of poker?" Molly's grin spread wide. "He can never resist cards or betting. Am I right?"

"But what would I use for collateral to buy chips? I can't compete with Gordon. He's got money coming out his ears."

Chapter 51

Some husband, Maureen thought as she unzipped her dress and let it fall to the floor. It dropped like a puddle around her bare feet.

James, still fully clothed, was sleeping atop the bed. His eyelids slid open, and he stretched his arms. Unlike Maureen, he had always been able to hold his liquor. His vision landed on her face. "I must have dozed off." His gaze explored her curves. "This is not a complaint, but have you put on weight?"

"Too many desserts." Clad in her slip, Maureen's hands slid across her waistline, which had indeed grown rounder.

"Time to go on a diet so your suitors don't lose interest."

Her jaw tightened. "How dare you?"

"Hey, I saw how you and Gordon looked at each other."

"Gordon can look at me all day. I assure you nothing happened." Thank goodness. And thank goodness they'd located Amanda hiding behind a booth. Their daughter was sleeping with Lydia.

He put out his arms. "Come on in, baby. I'll warm you up."

She could never resist him. "Only if you promise to be faithful."

"Me?" He pushed himself to a sitting position, leaned against the headrest. "How about you?"

Maureen tried to look indignant but couldn't contain a smile. She stepped into her silk pajama bottoms and then buttoned up the top.

James patted the bed. "Come and keep daddy warm."

She hesitated.

"Have a better offer elsewhere?" he asked.

"No." She tried to recall the last time she and James had been together as man and wife. She hadn't bothered to use birth control because she was too old to get pregnant. Wasn't she? Her hands explored her round tummy as she did the math. After that hideous Christmas party. She would be only a couple of months along. And yet...

"Denny needs our help." Maureen decided to change the subject. His eyebrows raised. "You're worried about your little sister at a moment like this?"

"She needs money to keep her bookstore open. And to buy a puppy from Gordon."

"So I was right. What were you hoping to gain from getting into bed with him?"

"I'm not getting into bed with anyone but you." She stepped closer and snuggled into his outstretched arms.

"Do you even love me?" She was afraid of his answer.

"More than ever, Maureen."

"But Amanda told me—"

"You'd believe a teenage girl over your husband? She has a wild imagination."

He was right. Amanda had an overly active imagination. But Maureen needed to think clearly. Could she really be pregnant? Her job might be history anyway. But she did have a husband to love. Darn it all, she still adored James no matter what he'd done.

"Well, will you help Denny?" She stood akimbo.

"Anything you want." His mouth widened into a grin. "If you ask me, she needs more than money and a dog."

Maureen stiffened. "Please listen and take me seriously, just this once."

"I am listening, dearest darling. And I am taking you seriously. But I'm your husband and will not have my wife cavorting with another man, be he the owner of this hotel or not."

"Since when were you this concern about me?" she asked.

"Listen, it was no easy feat getting here through the snow,

and I see no show of gratitude." His voice turned gruff. "Are you happy to see me or not?"

"Yes, absolutely." The enormity of her situation smacked Maureen like a tsunami. If they split up could she raise a child on her own? Would Amanda help her? Lydia had hinted she needed to get back home, but Maureen could hire another Amish nanny or be a stay-at-home mom while she wrote her new book.

As she pondered her future, she moved into her husband's outstretched arms. She could feel his warmth.

A severe rapping on the door brought Maureen out of her contemplation. As she swung her legs over the side of the bed and stood James moaned, but Maureen ignored him. She wanted to see if Amanda, who'd hitchhiked back to the hotel earlier, needed anything. Maureen moved to the door and asked, "Who's there?"

"Me." Maureen recognized Denny's voice.

"Just a minute." Maureen slipped into a bathrobe, then opened the door.

"Okay for me to come in?" Denny seemed in distress.

"Of course." Maureen ignored James's groan emanating from the bed.

Once inside, Denny leaned against the door to close it. "Alec and Molly said they're definitely not getting married. But they are moving to the States together." Her statement hung in the air. "Now what should I do?"

"Do about what?" Maureen moved closer to her little sister. "How can I help?"

Denny spat out her statement. "I don't want your help, unless you can find a way to stop them from leaving together."

"Because?" Maureen took in Denny's tortured features and reality dawned. Maureen's sister had fallen hard for Alec.

"I don't get it," James said.

Maureen turned to him and said, "She doesn't want them to live together in any capacity."

"Then what do you want?" he asked.

Denny visibly shrank. Her face contorted and melted like a

wax mask. She let out a sob, then wiped her nose with the back of her sleeve. "Never mind."

"Pay no attention to him," Maureen said. "You know how dense men can be."

"Hey, I didn't come all this way to be insulted," James said.

"Sorry, dearest husband. That was not my intent."

Denny marveled at Maureen's finesse. She could wrap James around her little finger. When she wanted to.

"You've fallen in love with Alec, haven't you?" Maureen asked.

Denny bobbed her head.

"What on earth for?" James sounded perplexed. "Get real. I doubt he has any money."

"What does money matter in affairs of the heart?" Maureen cinched the waist of her bathrobe. "That's not why I love you." There, she'd said it. She loved James but knew he took advantage of that fact.

The corner of his mouth tugged up into a partial smile. "You have a strange way of showing that you love me. You're gone all the time, working at the studio. You're always too busy for me."

"I didn't think you noticed." Her face radiant, Maureen pivoted toward the bed and then sank into the covers next to him.

Denny turned away. "Guess I'd better give you two lovebirds your privacy back." Then she hastened out the door.

Chapter 52

Had Lydia ever felt lonelier? She doubted it. Not even when her friend Mary told her she hated her. Lydia still wasn't sure why but had to believe that Mary had a good reason. Lydia could think of many reasons to hate herself.

Her mind swirled like an undertow at the bottom of a waterfall at Ricketts Glen State Park, back in Pennsylvania—a three-hour drive to the north of the farm in a hired passenger van. Her family's yearly splurge, including tents, a small trailer to carry a week's worth of food—of course only when Dat could find help for the farm.

Always, she and Jonathan would conspire to camp the same week at the same location. Surely their parents had caught onto their antics because they expected the two to be wed. On those camping trips, often a dozen or so singles, including Lydia and Jonathan, would pair up and sneak away together into the shadows.

Lydia remembered the evening Jonathan first took her hand. His were large and manly. A warmth buzzed up her arm and landed in her heart. They walked together without speaking for ten minutes. Finally, in slow motion, he turned and kissed her. The earth stopped revolving as she'd luxuriated in his embrace.

But would he be repulsed if he found out the truth? That she was a thief and still struggled to remain honest?

She made a decision. She would not act impetuously as she had when traipsing off on this trip. What had she been thinking? She could be baptized and married by now.

Chapter 53

"Just so we're clear, Denny," Alec said when Molly had left the room. "Molly and I will never marry. We can't."

"Never?" Denny didn't buy it.

"Not ever." His face took on a mask of confusion. "We're forbidden to by law."

Denny was so done with this conversation. She knew better than to believe him, or any man. Only her father had she trusted to be straight with her—even if he had put her down now and then. Thinking of him made her stomach twist. Should she track down the person who'd killed her precious parents?

She turned to Alec and got honest. Not enough time for word games. "I may need your help."

"In what way?" His voice softened. "I know you want wee Rosie. And to venture out of Maureen's shadow. She would be a tough act to follow."

"And to find the drunk or stoned maniac who killed my parents, which seems impossible at this late date."

"You poor lass. What can I do to help?"

"Nothing and everything." Denny turned toward him. "I was lazy at the time of their deaths," she said. "I should have tried harder and been firmer with the police department."

He tilted his head. "I don't believe a woman who owns a bookstore can be lazy. And you ventured out in the snowstorm to carry wood. Not the act of a lazy woman."

"Only to be with you." Her hand flew up to cover her mouth. Why had she revealed her feelings?

"I'm flattered." His hand rose to his chest. "But I'm no great catch. Just a working man like any other."

She was moved by his humility. "I beg to differ," she said. "You're nothing like any other man I've met."

"Better or worse?" He lowered his face to gaze into her eyes, but she was too flustered to look back.

She squeezed her eyes shut. "Much, much better." Her throat tightened around her words.

"Seriously?" His voice turned upbeat. "In that case, please tell me more."

"Not much to tell." Denny felt heat rising up her throat and her cheeks no doubt turning red. She had no control over her own body. How embarrassing.

"What can I do to help?" he asked. His voice sounded sincere, but could she trust him?

She opened her eyes and found him staring into her face. "What do you know about running a book business?" she asked.

"Not much, although I enjoy reading. And my business is in the black when it isn't snowing."

"You mean it's going out of business?"

"Quite the contrary. I'm doing so well that my chief competitor offered to buy my fleet. And I accepted his offer." He stroked his jaw. "When Molly talked of moving to America with her, I said okay."

"Why is she moving?" Denny didn't trust Molly or her motivations. And why would Alec give up everything to be with her?

"So she can study nursing," he said.

"She wants to become a nurse? Why cross the ocean to go to nursing school?"

Denny realized she was talking down about Molly without good reason. Jealousy was Denny's problem. She might as well admit she had a crush on Alec. Denny looked up into his wonderful face and could not see how their relationship would work.

"Molly's a clever lass." Alec said. "She doesn't want to wait on tables in a hotel her whole life."

"Understandable." The question that was pressing in on

Denny sailed out of her mouth. "So you two are *not* planning to get married?"

Alec chuckled. "That would be like marrying my sister. Never going to happen." He stepped closer. "Especially when my heart belongs to you."

"Me?" Denny was bamboozled. She felt the same way about him, but no way could it work out. "I've got to be straight with you." She could barely admit it to herself. "I may be very sick." She could tell by his facial expression that she'd captured his full attention. "Nothing contagious," she said.

He waited for her to finish. "Then what?" he finally asked. "If I'm not being too nosy."

Denny let out all her breath. It felt good to open up to Alec. "The tests have shown nothing so far and I continue to have abdominal pain at night. I came to Skye before I could find out the latest results of the most recent tests."

"You should call your doctor today. Or ask Molly what to do."

Molly stepped into the room. "Did I hear my name? Are you two talking about me?"

"You'd help our Denny track down her medical records, would you not?"

Molly's continence turned severe. "She can't locate her own medical records? I find this hard to believe."

"Now Molly," Alec said, "not everyone is as at home in the medical world as you are."

"If you insist." Molly glanced at her watch. "I'll get right on it as soon as her doctor's office opens." She put her flattened hand out to Denny and said, "I'll need to impersonate you if you don't mind my pretending to be you."

"Not in the slightest." In spite of her false bravado, Denny was still hesitant. Fear clutched her like a strait jacket, making it hard to move freely. She tried to look at ease, but her mind flailed with trepidation, which she had stashed on the back burner.

"Give me a couple of hours." Molly stared into Denny's face. "Are you sure you want to know?"

Kate Lloyd

"Good question. But the answer is yes." She had been longing to hear the truth, no matter. Or so she'd thought.

Kate Lloyd

204

Chapter 54

Gordon opened his bedroom door with a flourish and spoke to Maureen as she made her way to the kitchen for a glass of milk. "Wait, Maureen, my beauty, come here."

Deep in thought, she stopped so quickly that she almost tripped. Nothing good could come from a conversation with Gordon unless he broke down and sold her the puppy that Denny wanted. Maureen could not imagine desiring a little dog so much, but she knew her younger sister was lonely.

When she heard heavy footsteps striding toward her, she spun around and spotted James lumbering down the hallway. He appeared incensed, his eyes bulging like the bull that she'd seen on a TV show about the Wild West. "My wife is none of your concern." He balled his fist and looked ready for another wrestling match.

"Now, now, don't get all worked up over nothing." Gordon produced a smile. "As you can see, your lovely wife is safe and sound." He massaged his hands together. "James, can I interest you in a friendly game of cards?"

"I suppose so." James had won Maureen's Lexus in a poker game, but she had no idea how much money he'd lost to his Friday night poker buddies over the years.

"She took hold of James's forearm. "Are you sure, darling?"

James yanked his arm away and moved into Gordon's bedroom. "Got anything to drink?" he asked Gordon.

"Of course I do. This is a full-service hotel. Nothing but the best." He backstepped into a spacious and opulent room with an oversized wooden desk. "I have a bottle of the very finest scotch right here."

From the hallway, Maureen watched Gordon pour two drinks. Then he brought out a fresh deck of cards. Facing each other, the two men sat at a table. Maureen wished James wasn't gambling, but she hoped he'd be the winner. Gordon shuffled the cards and offered them to James to cut. She couldn't bear to watch any longer.

Her mind gyrated with uncertainty. In the past, she'd wondered if her husband had drinking and gambling addictions—much like her father had, if honest with herself. Is that where their parents' money went? Online gambling or wagers at the golf course? She reminded herself that her husband, James was a highly respected trial attorney at a prestigious law firm. And James had assured her his Friday night poker buddies weren't addicts. "It's like playing golf," he'd said, as if she were insane. "A competitive sport, but all in good fun."

Thirty minutes later, Maureen peeked through the cracked door opening into the room and saw the two men hunkered at the table, cards in hand—held close to their chests.

She felt a thrill as she accepted the fact that her husband loved her. She had long given up that dream. And she might be pregnant with his child. Certainly no other man's. Thank goodness she had not succumbed to Gordon's overtures. She would still write her cookbook, and it would be a smash hit bestseller. She envisioned her book signing in technicolor.

A warmth pervaded her when she realized how full her life was. She leaned against the wall outside of Gordon's room. She closed her eyes and visualized the cover of her future book, adorned with delectable edibles from the British Isles, and inside, the recipes with mouth-watering color photos. Yes, this hotel was the perfect venue. But more than anything, she wanted to have her family reunited. And that included Denny. If she could just give Denny her heart's desire, maybe their fractured relationship would be forever mended.

Men's voices erupted from Gordon's room, then the air fell silent. Maureen speculated about what was happening but knew better than to interrupt James. She'd made that mistake before and had received a royal dressing down.

A couple of hours later, the door opened. James poked his head out and grinned at her.

Chapter 55

"Ta-da. I won big-time." James moved over to Maureen and hugged her. A sloppy hug. She leaned back to avoid his breath, reeking of liquor. "This hotel is now ours. Yours and mine, sugar."

"Live here? Do you mean to tell me that you plan to move us to Scotland and make this hotel our permanent home?" she asked. "But—but we already have a home. And a membership to the country club." Her mind explored the possibilities. She saw herself greeting travelers, that she might call *our guests*, and overseeing the menu. She'd be a queen again instead of a nobody. Again. But she said, "How can you be happy about taking another man's livelihood away from him? Not to mention his stature in the community."

"Okay, I hear you, but we could visit once a year. Under all that snow, there must be a golf course or two."

Maureen was speechless. She'd wanted a vacation home on Martha's Vineyard or Nantucket—not on the other side of the Atlantic Ocean.

"Why aren't you smiling, sugar?" James asked.

"Because all I wanted from Gordon is a little cairn terrier puppy. The one my sister adores—when it's old enough to leave its mother.

Maureen had never seen James look so flabbergasted. His cheeks turned the color of a ripe tomato. "Are you serious?" he asked, and she nodded. "Now I've heard it all. Are you going through the change of life?"

"No." She rubbed her tummy. "Not yet."

"I ordinarily give you everything you want, but this is too much."

She was determined not to give in. "We can still visit. Next time during the summer. Maybe go to St. Andrews. Isn't that where you'd rather be? Golf where all the greatest golfers in the world long to play."

"I suppose they might have nice places to stay there too. If you promise not to get on my case for golfing all the time."

"I promise I won't, darling."

"What about your phenomenal career?"

"I would give that up for you today." She knew she was being duplicitous, but she wasn't ready to admit the calamity on her television show or how she was directed to keep off the set until the newspaper frenzy blew over. If it did. In days James would read about her.

He tugged his earlobe, then he spun around and stomped back into Gordon's room. Minutes later he stepped through the doorway again. "Don't ever claim I don't do anything for you. I just traded this valuable hotel for a crummy little dog." James shook his head. "I must be going nuts."

"You did? Really?" Maureen clung onto the tangible proof that he loved her. "Thank you so much, darling," she said.

"It seems I can't win with you." He shook his head. "I'm never good enough. Always something wrong."

"Not true," Maureen said. "You're my knight in shining armor."

"You have a strange way of showing it. You're always in competition with me and coming out the winner."

Already Maureen started second-guessing herself. Had she made a mistake?

"I'm sorry, my dearest husband. I didn't mean to be disrespectful." Maureen spoke up to James in a subservient manner. "You will be my husband forever. The father of our child. And maybe our future baby. Would you mind another child?"

He seemed to inflate. "Mind? Are you kidding? I'd be thrilled."

"Well, I might already be pregnant."

"But how could you know? Have you gone to a doctor?"

"No, but I've been having the weirdest cravings—the way I did when I was carrying Amanda."

"Amanda can be our babysitter."

"Maybe, but you know our Amanda." Maureen scanned the hall.

"I hope it's a boy this time," James said. "Too many women in our family." James wrapped his arms around her and kissed her lips in a way that brought back memories of their wedding night when love was fresh and alive.

After they stepped apart, Gordon strode out into the hall and slapped James on the back as if they were old friends. "I can't thank you enough," Gordon said. "I will always be in your debt."

"You've got that right."

Chapter 56

For a few minutes Lydia toyed with the idea of staying here on the Isle of Skye and working in the hotel. She loved the place. Maybe she could use a room like the one Alec occupied. She wouldn't mind sleeping in the basement one bit.

"Lydia, dear, I found that missing money exactly where I hid it," Mrs. Ross had admitted earlier. "It seems the older I get the more forgetful I am. You really are a sweet lass. Please forgive me."

"Of course, it's already done." Lydia was delighted to bestow the gift she longed for.

She had proven herself to Mrs. Ross, although not to the owner, the decision maker. She would have to speak to the man who had a reputation of being belligerent and negative. Fear inundated her. She couldn't face meeting him.

Feeling alone and despondent, Lydia saw no chance of regaining her nanny job once this trip was over, which was no doubt for the best. Lydia would return to the farm in defeat. But her parents, the bishop, ministers, deacons, and all who lived in her district would forgive and accept her. Yet would Jonathan still love her once he found out about her transgressions? Unlikely.

Lydia knew this Englisch life was not for her. How could she expect her future children to resist temptation if she couldn't manage it herself?

When she envisioned Jonathan in another woman's arms, she recoiled. Her choices had been all wrong, and she deserved punishment. Life without love and a family would be a punishment as bad as being imprisoned. If she didn't return, her parents would be disgraced.

211

Lydia longed to breathe in the farmland aromas of freshly mown hay and newly harvested corn in the crib. She missed her parents and siblings, aunts and uncles, her many cousins, the whole congregation of about two hundred. All would look after her. She envisioned Dat's silo as tall as the giant oak tree out behind their two-story home. She missed riding in his buggy. The sound of their mare's clopping hooves and the buggy's metal wheels on the asphalt roads. When it snowed in Lancaster County, she would sit with Mam and crochet before the hearth. A robust fire would send heat into the room.

On cold nights, Jonathan could keep her warm—once they were married. If he still loved her. If he didn't, so be it. She had made her bed and must sleep in it, as Dat would say.

Climbing the hotel's carpeted stairs, Lydia felt winded, her energy depleted. She stood for a moment catching her breath. As if the clouds parted and the snow had eased up, Lydia could see clearly now. She wanted to go home to her parents more than anything, even if Jonathan didn't want her anymore. She must return to her Amish community.

She brought out her cell phone and texted him. But his sister texted in return telling Lydia that he had lent her his phone. *Jonathan's not here. My bruder did his chores and is now helping widow Sarah and her three children. He's been spending a great deal of time with her lately.* Spending time with widow Sarah newly arrived from Kentucky. Lydia knew Jonathan was a hard worker and often volunteered to help neighbors, but she was engulfed with a feeling that he was more than helping her. As Lydia recalled, this graceful and attractive woman owned a great deal of real estate and a couple dozen milking cows, not to mention a thoroughbred buggy horse. And could she pour on the charm. Lydia could see her green eyes that echoed a hand-sewn dress and apron with even stitches. And her organza white heart shaped cap was always pressed to perfection. Lydia assumed that Sarah was looking for a husband and could beguile her Jonathan. Not that Jonathan was Lydia's by any means. Lydia hadn't even been baptized into the Amish church. And she certainly wasn't living an Amish life.

She sighed as she thought of how easily men were beguiled. She couldn't wait to get home—the sooner the better. She no longer wanted a terrier but rather a herding dog to look after a small flock of sheep that she hoped to own with Jonathan. And a goat or two for milking and making yogurt. She could almost taste its creaminess.

When had that dream died, and why had she left Lancaster County? Looking back at her far-fetched decisions, Lydia realized sin had let her astray. She shuddered when she considered what power her transgressions had over her. She needed to return and confess no matter the consequences.

Lydia reminded herself that very few in the Amish community were shunned if they repented and confessed. She needed to take the classes and be baptized into the Amish church. Even if Jonathan married another woman, her parents would be ecstatic.

Chapter 57

Denny grinned as she realized she hadn't experienced abdominal pain or thought about her discomfort all day. Dwelling on her problem hadn't improved her health, but something had. For a moment she considered staying on the Isle of Skye. But her bookstore wouldn't survive without her. And what fun would staying be without Alec here? She was growing more and more fond of him. No, make that she had the hots for him big time. But could she trust any man? What was his relationship with Molly all about? She decided to find Molly and speak to her woman to woman. Before she could move, she saw Maureen striding toward her.

"I have a giant surprise for you." Maureen reminded Denny of a cat who'd swallowed the canary. As pleased as punch.

"Now what?"

"My James won your puppy for you. Rosie is now yours."

"No way." Denny wouldn't get her hopes up.

"Yes, way. I'm serious, little sister."

Denny wasn't buying into her story. She stood looking into Maureen's elated face. Was this a cruel hoax? Typical of James.

"Come on," Maureen said. "Show a little gratitude already."

"Okay, I'll play along with your story. James had a complete personality reversal." But Denny wouldn't believe it. She'd been hurt too often.

"Yeah, I hear you. I was surprised too." Maureen moved closer. "My dearest, darling husband won Rosie in a card game with Gordon. James gave up owning this valuable hotel for you. For me really. Because I asked him to."

"I'll have to see it to believe it."

"And I'm pregnant."

"No way." Denny assessed Maureen's curvaceous figure. Her older sister's tummy was rounded but Denny assumed she'd eaten too much. "At your age? Are you sure?"

"Yes, my daughter brought a home pregnancy test along in her suitcase."

"Why on earth?" Denny hadn't even gone out on a date at Amanda's age.

"I don't know what she was thinking would happen on this trip. That she'd age ten years and meet Prince Charming?" Maureen shook her head once. "More evidence that I need to spend more time at home with Amanda."

"Have you told James?" Denny had heard of midlife babies. Maybe Maureen was having a midlife crisis.

"Yes, and he's over-the-moon ecstatic about it. As am I."

"I'm happy for you." Denny would have another niece or nephew.

"James wants me and Amanda to come home with him tomorrow morning," Maureen said. "He's heard the snow is going to turn into rain as the temperature goes up. And we'll take Lydia with us too. And of course, you, my little sister."

"So soon?" Denny was caught off guard. She wasn't ready to leave, but she could see no way out of her dilemma of possibly never seeing Alec again. Did she even have time to say goodbye to him?

"Think of it—in a private jet all to ourselves." Maureen's mouth curved into a smile. "I've got to run. James is waiting for me." She flew up the stairs.

Denny quaked as she watched Maureen's departing form and envisioned her sister slipping into bed with James.

"Whatever," Denny said, feeling empathy and gratitude for Maureen.

Maureen turned for a moment and said, "You'll come with us, won't you?"

"Yeah, I guess so." Did Denny have any choice?

As if waiting in the wings, Molly cruised over to Denny. "I hear we'll be delivering your puppy." Molly's eyes flashed.

"We?"

"Yes, Alec and I."

"Please tell me the truth." Denny tried to mask the whimper in her voice. "Are you two an item? Meaning a couple."

"Heavens, no." Molly sputtered a laugh. "Not that I don't love Alec like a brother."

"Humph." Denny had seen how easily the two interacted. Envy filled her, which was dumb. Yet her attraction to him was like a magnet to steel. And she hoped he felt the same way about her.

"I promise you it's true." Molly took Denny's hand. "Why would I lie to you? And I come bearing good news for which I am genuinely happy." She dropped Denny's hand. "I have a question for you."

Denny's curiosity was tweaked, but she kept her face from revealing it. "What?"

"Your pain. Have you considered your diet? I got online and saw in your doctor's notes that you might have irritable bowel syndrome. I read an article only last week about how it can be managed by a change of diet." She grinned exposing pearly white teeth. "I'll prepare your meals for you as long as you're staying at the hotel."

"Why would you do that?"

"I'm hoping you'll let me stay with you in New Jersey," Molly said. "Until I move into the dorms—I'm on a waiting list— or until I find a place of my own."

"Why would you want to live there?" Denny had a spare bedroom and plenty of closet space. But what a weird request from a woman she barely knew.

"There's a nursing school at Rutgers University in New Jersey," Molly said. "I've already been accepted there with a partial scholarship. And I've been saving up my money."

"Let me give it some thought." Denny already knew her answer would be no, even if it meant she'd spend more time with Alec. He'd promised to deliver Rosie in person, but would that fairytale come to fruition? Highly unlikely. A thud of disappointment hit the pit of her stomach. She knew failure awaited her.

"I'll do the cooking," Molly said. "A rotation diet, only food that will sooth your painful condition away. And I'll do the laundry while you're at work. And clean up your apartment until it sparkles. And help with the puppy if need be."

Molly's declaration was hard to ignore. Denny had been in such a hurry when she'd left for this trip her apartment was in disarray. Dirty dishes soaking in soapy water waited in the sink, soiled clothes lay in heaps by the washing machine and in her bedroom. And hadn't there been nights when she longed for company?

"Molly, if you're being straight with me, the answer then is yes."

"Thank you. I look forward to making my first patient pain free."

Molly cleared her throat as Alec approached. "Alec, would you please tell Denny that we're just friends? She's got this crazy notion."

Denny held her breath and waited.

"How can we convince you?" Alec's gaze locked onto Denny's. "We're cousins, childhood best friends. Nothing more."

"Cousins?"

"Aye, first cousins. I thought you knew. Mrs. Ross told me she'd explained it to you."

"No, she never said a thing." Denny felt glimmers of hope and trust. She acted as if his words meant nothing to her when in truth she was ready to jump up and down, clap her hands, and yell, "Yay!"

"I just heard the good news from Gordon himself." Alec looked into Denny's face with intensity. "I'm not sure how it all

217

came about, but he said he's giving you Rosie and has entrusted me to bring her to the States when she's two months old."

Denny felt weak in the knees. Were her dreams coming true? She was used to having the rug pulled out from under her.

She wanted to yell "Shut up!" to the negative voices nattering in her ears as if demons were perched on her shoulders. But if she did, Alec would think she was a kook. Maybe she was to think she'd find happiness here on the Isle of Skye.

She glanced out a window and saw descending drops of water. She stepped closer to watch the rain drizzling down. The snow on the ground was melting, leaving behind slush and puddles.

"This is our typical Scottish weather," Alec said. "We never know from day to day. However, snow down at this level of the island is rare. We normally get rain." He rolled his *r*'s.

"We get lots of snow in New Jersey," Denny said, not wanting to talk about the weather. "Did you know that Molly asked to stay with me until she gets a place of her own, and I said okay. She'll do the cooking. Some kind of rotation diet until we figure out what's wrong with me."

"That's very kind of you." He stood so close Denny was tempted to kiss him. "But it leaves me out in the cold," he said. "Where will I stay?"

"I have a couch that pulls out into a bed you could sleep on." Denny surprised herself with her own audacity. "It's not comfortable. And we'll be a little tight in my apartment."

"That seems like a terrible imposition."

Denny wondered if she was being played for a fool, but she wanted to explore their relationship further. "I warn you, I'll put you to work in my bookstore," she said. "Can you build bookshelves?"

"Yes. I can build fine bookshelves. And I'll sand and stain them."

"And help me in my shop, moving and rearranging books? Dust and spruce up the place."

"Anything you wish. It will be like a second chance for me to better myself." Alec's face filled with elation.

Denny wanted to ask his intentions with her but felt too shy.

Chapter 58

After their private jet took off, leaving the Isle of Skye, the Gulfstream G800 muscled its way through pouring rain, turbulence, and was soon soaring above the clouds.

Maureen got on her phone and called the TV network. "I'm sorry, but your show's been cancelled," an executive said. Sure enough they had given her the boot before she even got home. "You understand, don't you?" he said. "We wish you well."

"Not a problem." Maureen felt as though she was starting a new beginning. A reinvigorated marriage, a child on the way, and a new career.

"I have other plans," Maureen told him. New and better plans. "I was going to hand in my resignation anyway." No need to mention her pregnancy or book deal yet.

Her new agent, Lucinda Lastrange, who represented only clients with star-studded potential, was delighted to take Maureen on. "Once your baby's born and your book is planned out, we'll take you to new heights," Lucinda assured her on their initial phone conversation. The sky's your limit."

Now for possibly the toughest conversation with her daughter, who sat next to her peering out the window. "You and I need to talk," she said to Amanda. "I've got exciting news. Unless I am mistaken, you're soon to have a baby brother or sister."

"I'd be okay with it." Amanda kept her seatbelt fastened. "I hope it's a girl. No, a baby brother might be fun."

"I'll be working from home from now on."

"To keep a better eye on me?" Amanda rolled her eyes in the way that always aggravated Maureen. "Or an excuse to fire Lydia?"

Maureen was onto her daughter's scare tactics. "No, to spend more time together. In fact, Lydia gave me notice yesterday. She wants to move home to her family in Lancaster County. She suggested I hire her friend, but I said, 'No thanks, I want to be a stay-at-home mom.'"

"So you can spy on me?" Amanda's voice was laced with sarcasm.

"No, I want to spend more time with you. I enjoyed our time together. I realized I wasted years." Maureen was speaking from her heart. "In the blink of an eye, you'll be flying off to college, and then the world is your oyster." Community college might be a better goal, but no need to mention her predictions.

"I don't like oysters, and you know it. Don't you know anything about me?"

"Probably not as much as Lydia does, and it's no one's fault but my own. I only hope I can help you with your homework as well as Lydia did." It wouldn't hurt Maureen to expand her own education. "At one time I was a good student, but that was a long time ago."

"Whatever. If you say so."

"I do say so. I'm still your mother." Maureen would not be her daughter's pushover anymore.

Chapter 59

"Thanks for driving me home—and everything." As Lydia said her goodbyes and exited Maureen's car, heady farmland fragrances engulfed her. She felt as if she were finally reaching shore after drifting at sea aimlessly like a chunk of wood. She breathed to her fullest. She noticed laundry hanging on the line and was grateful she'd kept her dresses, aprons, and white heart-shaped cap. Even the straight pins holding her garments together.

When she arrived at Jonathan's parents' farm, she was filled with anticipation and a case of nerves. She tied the mare to a hitching post and climbed the steep stairs to the back porch bedecked with a lawn swing and chairs. She couldn't resist sitting on the swing for a moment to admire the grand fields that seemed to spread forever. The melody of birds trilling and warbling filled her ears.

She noticed movement in the distance and recognized Jonathan turning over the soil using his dat's four giant Percherons—preparing the earth to plant acres and acres of corn. If they wed, Lydia would be expected to assist him, a task she would gladly take on.

She descended the steps and went to Jonathan. Intent on his work, he didn't notice her until she called out, "I'm home, Jonathan."

He steadied his horse and glanced her way but said nothing.

She sprinted across to his side. "Can you ever forgive me?" she asked.

"That depends." He jiggled the reins, and the horses moved forward.

She struggled to keep up with him. "I implore you to please wait."

He stopped his team but kept a tight grip on the reins. "Are you staying for good?" he asked.

"Yes. Even if you've given up on me." She waited for a sign of affection but saw only blue eyes glaring back at her.

Chapter 60

Denny unlocked her little bookstore, wedged between two larger businesses—a bakery and a hardware store. She felt like a stranger in her own shop.

She scanned down the aisles and attempted to see it the way a customer would. With stacks of books in the aisles, *disheveled* and *homely* were the words that came to mind. She could cry. She reprimanded herself for ever leaving it in Agnes's care. Because only Denny loved this little bookstore. As she sorted through a pile of books, she recalled the day she'd arrived, and the unsettling phone call the hotel had received from a couple named Campbell, who were not impersonating her parents. Turned out they were stuck in a tour bus on the other side of the icy bridge and only wished to cancel their reservations.

And if Denny hadn't gone to the Isle of Skye, she never would have met Alec. There was no getting around the fact that she loved him.

The store's landline phone rang, startling Denny. She picked it up and said, "Hello, the Open Book."

"Denny," Alec said, "I just wanted to hear your voice. I miss you fiercely."

"I feel the same way." Denny's patience was being put to the test.

"I can't wait to see you. I'm counting the days."

Denny looked at the wall clock. "I'm counting the hours."

Epilogue: One Year Later

Denny and Alec's wedding is everything she'd hoped for and more. Thanks to Lydia's Amish connection, Denny and Alec arrive at the chapel in a horse-drawn buggy.

Lydia returned to Lancaster County with humility to her Amish community where she was welcomed back by her parents and everyone in their church district. Maybe not with hugs and kisses, but then her dat and her mam never even hugged each other in public. Then the next day her father and their Amish bishop visited the shoe store, paid for the stolen shoes out of Lydia's earned wages, and insisted the owner write Paid in Full on the receipt.

Denny is wowed by how handsome Alec is wearing his kilt. Gordon, also clad in a kilt, flew over the Atlantic Ocean to walk Denny down the aisle. He and James have become genuine friends since Gordon fell in love with a local Scottish lass. Once standing before the pastor, Denny notices Lydia sitting in the first pew row with her new husband, Jonathan, and Molly, now thriving in nursing school. Across the aisle, Maureen sits with James, who jiggles his and Maureen's infant, a boy they named Robert after Denny and Maureen's deceased father. Behind is a roomful of friends and family members, both Amish and English. Standing room only.

Amanda is the flower girl. She carries Rosie as she solemnly walks forward. Thankfully Rosie is sleeping. She's a rambunctious cairn terrier pup who has brought Denny much joy.

"Who needs rose petals when we have the real thing?" Denny asked Maureen a couple of weeks ago.

"Whatever you decide," Maureen said. "It's your wedding. Yours and Alec's, that is." Maureen graciously oversaw the flowers and catered food for the sit-down reception dinner for two hundred at the nearby country club.

The two sisters hugged each other.

"I love you, Maureen," Denny said, her heart free of resentment and full of forgiveness.

"I love you too," Maureen echoed. "Forever."

Today a bagpipe outside the chapel plays an uplifting melody that stirs Denny's soul. She and Alec will visit the Isle of Skye on their honeymoon. She can't wait to explore the whole island with Alec as her tour guide.

Denny's little bookshop is thriving now that its owner is invigorated and free from pain, thanks to Molly's cooking and sage advice, the devotion of a loving husband who works by her side, and her saucy cairn terrier, Rosie.

Maureen's Snicker Doodle Recipe

1/2 cup softened butter
1 cup sugar
1 large egg, room temperature
1/2 teaspoon vanilla extract
1-1/2 cups all-purpose flour
1/4 teaspoon salt
1/4 teaspoon baking soda
1/4 teaspoon cream of tartar

CINNAMON SUGAR:
2 tablespoons sugar
2 teaspoons ground cinnamon

1. Preheat oven to 375°. Cream butter and sugar until light and fluffy; beat in egg and vanilla. In another bowl, whisk together flour, salt, baking soda and cream of tartar; gradually beat into creamed mixture.

2. In a small bowl, combine sugar and cinnamon. Shape dough into 1-in. balls; roll in cinnamon sugar. Place 2 in. apart on ungreased baking sheets.

3. Bake until light brown, 10-12 minutes. Remove from pans to wire racks to cool. Makes two and half dozen.

Acknowledgments

Mega gratitude to my readers. I appreciate each one of you more than you can ever know! I wish I could thank my father, the late Professor John Brodie McDiarmid, in person. He often talked about his Scottish heritage, took us to the Highland Games, and traveled with me throughout Scotland. Thank you to my dear sister, Margaret Coppock, for her encouragement and for providing me with a contact in Scotland who helped update me on the changes since the last time I visited the Isle Skye. Not to mention sharing her expertise of the English language and recollections of our father driving on the wrong side of the road. She is the only person who can make me laugh until I cry. Thank you to my Webmaster, Lisa-Ann Oliver of Web Designs by LAO, for lending me her grandmother's recipe for Snickerdoodles. Thanks to my copy editor, Kathy Burge. Thank you to Margaret Durkee for sharing her Scottish family history with me. Many thanks to Lori Wilen for proofreading and helping me design my book cover. We enjoyed many a fun chat! Thank you to proofreader, Sarah Williams. Many thanks to Judi Fennell at formatting4U for her patience and formatting skills. Finally, I am indebted to Mary Jackson, AKA @themaryreader! Please forgive me if I forgot anyone, which no doubt I did.

I love hearing from readers!

Visit my Website where you can sign up for my Newsletter and find out about future Giveaways https://www.katelloyd.com

Please follow me on Instagram @katelloydauthor

Facebook: https://www.facebook.com/katelloydbooks/

I love hearing from readers! Please leave a short online review. I learn so much from them.

About The Author

Kate Lloyd is a novelist and a passionate observer of human relationships. A native of Baltimore, she and her husband live in the Pacific Northwest, the setting of several of her novels. She lived in Rome and studied Italian in college. Kate has worked a variety of jobs, including car salesman and restaurateur.

Learn more about Kate on her website:
https://www.katelloyd.com
Her blog: http://katelloydauthor.blogspot.com
Face Book: www.facebook.com/katelloydbooks
Instagram: @katelloydauthor
Pinterest: KateLloydAuthor

Made in United States
Troutdale, OR
10/01/2024

23302159R00133